The Brazos Legacy

The white men called him Lee Fargo and the Comanche named him Tall Wolf. He was a man of two tribes yet belonged to neither.

Torn from the only life he had known for sixteen years, he was thrown into a new kind of violence, hatred and deception that threatened his very existence. All he could do was fight back the only way he knew how: meet violence with greater violence and treachery with cunning. It would indeed be an eye for an eye.

And in the end, reeking of blood and gunsmoke, he belonged to no one and had no place to go.

The Brazos Legacy

TYLER HATCH

A Black Horse Western

ROBERT HALE · LONDON

ISBN 0 7090 7075 6

Robert Hale Limited
Clerkenwell House
Clerkenwell Green
London EC1R 0HT

WES
1303228

Typeset by
Derek Doyle & Associates, Liverpool.
Printed and bound in Great Britain by
Antony Rowe Limited, Wiltshire

1

White Savage

Most of the experienced warriors were away with Kiowa allies, forming a huge raiding party, terrorizing and slaughtering white settlers in lonely areas of the Brazos country, so there was not much activity among the tipis in the camp by the wide river.

The village was guarded by young up-and-coming warriors, inexperienced youths, not yet blooded by battle. Their job was to protect the women and children and the old men now too infirm to follow the blood-singing path of war. There was no reason why the village should expect an attack: the Comanche had ruled this country for centuries and remained rulers by force of arms.

But something had happened far, far to the north, in Montana, at a place called the Little Bighorn, only a couple of weeks earlier, on 25 June, in this year of 1876.

Custer and the Seventh Cavalry had made their Last Stand. More than 200 soldiers died at the hands of the Sioux and Cheyenne. The news of the massacre and

Indian triumph had shocked and then infuriated a nation.

Orders had gone out to the frontier army: *Avenge Custer! Kill all Indians on sight – male, female and children. Custer must be avenged!*

So, while the tribes of the Brazos had managed to escape the wrath of the white man's soldiers for many years – apart from the bitter, though brief Red River War of 1875 – going about their business on the southern plains, living the way of the Old Ones, that time had now ended. . . .

Sam'l Houston Noble was one of the best scouts the army had ever used. He was civilian and hired-out only when he needed money or when the buffalo had made their annual trek away from the Staked Plains and the Palo Duro, or when the gold he sought in the slow seasons proved too elusive for his pick and prospecting dish.

Noble was a man in his late fifties, had lived all his life in the wilderness, eschewed the company of men much of the time but made contact with them when necessary. Men and women – again, when necessary, although he was more partial to the Indian women than some of the white harlots who were the only ones available to him. 'Fact was, he enjoyed the company of wild things more than humans, and often he had been described as being more animal than man.

Noble took that as a compliment.

But now his pockets were empty and his clothes were ragged and his belly had never been really full for months. He needed army pay once again. And his timing was right.

'Hell, Sam, you couldn't've come at a better time,' said the colonel at Fort Griffin. 'Custer's been butchered along with a couple of hundred of his men up north – orders are to wipe the grins off the hostiles' faces once and for all. We need good scouts and I've always regarded you as one of the best.'

Noble stood tall, although his shoulders were hunched a mite these days. He was dressed in worn and greasy buckskin and a coonskin fur cap from which protruded long, silver hair curling down to his shoulders. His beard was long and fouled with food and twigs and leaves and – the colonel quietly speculated – likely a good deal of crawling wildlife. And he smelled to high heaven, but it was the smell of the wilds and would stand him in good stead when he was scouting for the Indians.

'Need grub and ammo and a better rifle than mine,' Noble said, his voice sounding strained: it was months since he had used it apart from cussing at some frustration in the wilds. He rapped the old Sharps carbine slung on a dogclip at his rawhide belt. 'Breech is cracked and nearly blinded me with a blow-by.'

The colonel was busy writing as Noble spoke and now waved the square of paper so as to dry the ink and handed it to the scout. 'Take it to the quartermaster – he'll give you whatever you need. Then report back to me and I'll have orders for you. . . .'

Noble stared down at the colonel. 'Same rate? Or has Wash'ton seen fit to raise the pay for a man who risks his scalp for little more'n bacon an' beans?'

The soldier smiled wearily: it was an old routine, had to be endured every time he hired a civilian for whatever purpose. 'I believe we can improve on last time, Sam.'

'Wouldn't be hard,' Noble growled, and left the office almost silently on his worn moccasins, only his rifle clip clicking a little.

The colonel sat back and linked his fingers, resting his chin upon them. He smiled slightly.

'Now you red bastards will pay for what you did to my old friend, George Armstrong Custer! You'll have to get up mighty early to outwit Sam'l Houston Noble! Yessir!'

But even a scout as good as Noble can make a mistake.

And he did.

Thing was, he didn't realize it. He had picked up a Yellow Boy Winchester repeating rifle from the quartermaster at Fort Griffin and, of course, the brass breech plate was highly polished, thereby giving the weapon its nickname. Moving silently as any snake in the brush on the slope above the Comanche village, he eased the rifle up alongside him, pulled it in front of his face and, as a precaution, slowly levered a shell into the breech. Then he let down the cocked hammer silently.

All this time, the brass plate had been catching a fugitive ray of sunlight slanting through the leaves of the white oaks and ash and hickory. Down in the village, one of the youthful guards – who took his job very seriously – was standing outside the tipi of Pretty Hair, wife of the tribal chief, Five Bears. Something caught his attention on the slope amongst the trees and brush. It flashed like gold, several times.

He was called Rain Lover and his heart suddenly hammered his ribcage as he fingered his short flatbow with the arrow already nocked but not yet drawn. His breath hissed in through bared teeth and he looked around swiftly, saw four of his companions lazing beneath a water elm, laughing and joking, perhaps one or two of them actually glad they had not been chosen for the war party.

Breathless now, he sauntered across to them as casually as he could, fighting to keep from glancing up at the clump of trees where he had seen the flash of light.

His friends saw him coming, started to joke with him until one, Tall Wolf, taller, straighter and leaner than the others, and with the suggestion of a light stubble along his jaw, saw Rain Lover's face and lifted a hand for an end to frivolity. The others frowned at this peremptory gesture.

'What ails you Rain Lover? Too many berries giving you a pain? Or is it pining for She Who Swims Like a Fish?'

That brought laughter to the others again and they joined in with jibes about the young maiden they knew Rain Lover coveted. But this time he didn't flush although there was a stammer in his voice when he spoke.

'The trees on the slope – take note of them without appearing to do so! I saw seven flashes of yellow light up there. We are being watched, perhaps by the white soldiers!'

That sobered the quartet, but they managed to refrain from glancing up the slope as they gathered their bows and quivers of arrows. A couple trembled visibly and their eyes stared wide at Rain Lover's news: soldiers meant terror and death.

'We must go as if we are moving to another lodge,' said the one called Tall Wolf. 'Move casually.'

The biggest youth, Like A Pine Tree, put a snarl into his voice, as he stood as straight as he could on his bow legs. 'Who are you to say what we should do?'

'It was a suggestion,' Tall Wolf said evenly, his blue eyes holding to Like A Pine Tree's until the youth glanced away. 'If we can keep the line of lodges between us and the slope, we can use the trees as cover and see for ourselves who made the flashes.'

One of the others groaned: the very thought that it might be white soldiers was now affecting them all.

'Yes, we will do that – I have decided!' snapped Like A Pine Tree, determined to assume command of the situation. 'We will find this white soldier who spies on us and we will torture him and get information to give Five Bears when he returns. He will reward us for our bravery and perhaps choose us to go on his next war party!'

Such thoughts swirled around inside their heads as Like A Pine Tree now led the way. Tall Wolf, silent, seemed content enough to follow – perhaps he was a little more easy-going than the others, did not feel the need to assert himself: after all, the suggestion to cover their movements had been his in the first place.

Or, perhaps it was simply that he wasn't as afraid as

the others. But if asked why, he would be unable to explain. Strangely, he had *never* been as awe-struck by the white invaders of *Comancheria* as the others of the tribe, full-fledged braves *or* novice-warriors.

It had puzzled him, but he had decided it was just something that was – *there*, within him. But privately, he admitted to himself, he was more afraid of white-eyed soldiers than of just one of the sorry-looking settlers living in a sod hut, trying to scrape a living out of the reluctant earth.

They wore fringed buckskin trousers and moccasins, with porcupine-quill breastplates and bands of painted rawhide around their heads. With arrows nocked, palms sweaty against the osage wood of the bows, they made their way into the cool shade of the trees. Following Rain Lover's shaky, pointing finger, they began to climb the slope towards the place where the flashes had been seen.

Sam Noble had watched the youths moving about the village, larking, jostling each other in the way of all young men feeling the sap of approaching adulthood singing in their veins. He watched casually, not giving them his full attention, squinted old eyes scanning the village, seeking older men, warriors, but in vain. He smiled thinly. *Looked like there was a war party gone off somewhere.* He tried to count the horses down in the holding ground but they moved around too much and it was partially hidden by a line of tipis anyway. But Noble was pretty damn sure he was right: just a few youngsters had been left to guard the women and children while the fighting men were away on some bloody business elsewhere.

The colonel and his troops, waiting three miles back, in a large canyon up-river, would be mightily pleased. The soldiers would swoop in with rifles, bayonets and sabres, and it would be a butcher's shop. It didn't bother Noble: he had lived in the wilds too long, had killed his share of Indians, had learned to respect them in some ways, but not enough to freeze him up if it came to a fight. Like most white men of his day, in his book, the only really good Indian was a dead Indian. . . .

It wasn't often that he underestimated a Comanche of any age – although he had been guilty of it twice and bore the scars and a stone arrowhead still grinding under his left shoulder blade to remind him of his mistake.

Now, getting old, he supposed, eyesight not what it used to be, reactions slowed down, he made the same mistake again: he dismissed the five youths he had seen down below as just a group of youngsters filling in time while the real warriors were off somewhere taking scalps and slaughtering settlers.

Until the first arrow zipped through the leaves and buried its stone head deep in his right thigh. It brought an involuntary cry from his tight throat but also jarred and honed his instincts. He slid away from the direction of attack, and two more arrows *twanged!* into the ground where he had lain stretched out. The Winchester came up and across his body and he triggered one-handed, the big gun jarring against his wrist, riding high high enough to smash the bullet through the middle of the face of Like A Pine Tree. As blood, bone and brains spattered the brush, the man behind let out a scream of terror and turned to run.

Noble shot him between the shoulders and he ploughed face first into the dirt of the slope. Rain Lover drew his bow and snapped a fast shot. The arrow sliced across Noble's left arm, hacking open a deep gash in the muscle. The rifle swayed and that shot went wild, but Noble rammed fumbling fingers through the lever and worked in another cartridge and fired before the arm and hand became completely numb.

Rain Lover spun and fell to one knee. The Indian behind him, running in for a shot with his bow, stumbled into the youth and somersaulted over his head. The fifth Comanche let out a blood-curdling yell and launched himself bodily at the old white man, drawing his hunting knife from its beaded buckskin sheath in mid-air.

His body weight crashed into Noble and bore the scout to the ground. Locked together, they slid down the slope while Tall Wolf, the one who had fallen over the dying Rain Lover, tried to fight off the reeling dizziness as blood ran down his face from where he had struck his head against a rock. Through a red curtain, he saw Noble rise uppermost and straddle the young Indian, twisting the knife from the brown hand with a cracking of finger bones that wrenched a yell from the Comanche. It was a yell that was replaced by a bubbling, dying scream as the scout plunged the knife into the young breast beneath the polished porcupine quill breastplate, shattering it as blood spurted.

Tall Wolf, groggy, wiped a hand across his eyes, blinking, trying to find his dropped bow and quiver of arrows. He found one arrow but the bow had slithered down the slope out of reach. Then he saw Noble lunging towards him, bloody knife in one hand, rifle in the other, face contorted in a snarling roar.

The young Indian felt the flood of fear surge through his taut body, wondering how he had ever failed to acknowledge the true fear of white men that lived deep within himself. Panicked, he fumbled for his knife. Then the scout was upon him, kicking him brutally in the chest, the savage force of the blow tearing loose the quill breastplate. It snapped the thin rawhide thongs that held it in place, and revealed the silver dollar with the eagle's feather dangling from a hole punched into the middle of the coin – an amulet to protect against bad medicine, resting against the pale skin of his chest.

Noble hesitated as awkwardly he levered a shell into the rifle's breech, blood streaming from his wounds, the arrow in his thigh broken now. Tall Wolf cowered as Noble leaned down towards him, yanked hard on the coin, snapping the thong.

Planting a grinding foot on the youth's chest, Noble examined the silver dollar which was dated fifteen years earlier, 1861. Something had been scratched deeply into the reverse side of the coin, like a letter R, resting on part of an arc. Noble snapped his head up, frowning down at the dazed, frightened youth. His broken teeth bared behind tightened lips.

'Boy, I am Sam'l Houston Noble. Now, that might not mean a goddamn thing to you right now, but I'm here to tell you that *I am your future!*'

And he raised the rifle and smashed the brass-bound butt between Tall Wolf's staring eyes.

2
Brazos Country
1884

Big Kent Rockwell farewelled his daughter, Liza, as usual, after supper outside the De Ville Restaurant in which he owned a half-share. It was a dark night, roiling black clouds blotting out the stars, and a cool, gusty wind blowing down Main Street.

Liza's skirts swirled about her legs and she put up a hand to hold on her hat. She was a fairly pretty young woman in her mid-teens, reddish hair blowing about her shoulders now. She smiled at her father.

'At least it's a relief from the heat.'

Rockwell grunted, turned his back, hunching up his big shoulders as he fired up a cigar. He turned back to the girl, patted her shoulder.

'Going to rain, and my guess is there'll be plenty of wildfire and thunder. You go straight to your room and I'll look in later.'

Her smile widened and there was a mischievous glint in her green eyes. 'Just to check that I'm there?'

'You know me better than that.' Kent Rockwell didn't have much of a sense of humour and saw little in life to make him rise to any light-hearted jibes, even from Liza on whom he doted. 'Just want to make sure you're safe and sound.'

'Father, I'm almost seventeen! You don't need to tuck me in any longer!' She lifted to her toes, still holding her hat with the other hand, and kissed him lightly on the cheek. 'But it's nice to know you care so much.'

'Go along now. Want Rip to walk with you?'

Her smile faded a little as she shook her head and said 'No!' with more emphasis than she meant to. 'I'll be fine.' She turned quickly and hurried along the boardwalk.

Kent stood looking after her a few moments, then pulled out a gold pocket watch, flipped open the cover, and grunted when he saw the time. After seven – he'd better hurry or the regular Thursday night poker group in the back of the Lone Star would be growing impatient. He owned a half-share in the saloon, too. In fact, he owned half of Santa Laga. . . .

He turned into the saloon, the batwings held open for him by a lean, hard-looking man with a narrow face and eyes to make a grizzly drop his stare. This was Rip Ohlrig, nominally Kent's foreman on the big Rocking R ranch, but mostly his troubleshooter and fixer.

As Ohlrig followed his boss into the saloon bar's wreath of smoke, he thought he heard a distant cry, but it was hard to tell with the wind blowing so hard and a rumble of thunder crashing across the sky. Then it started to rain, big, splattery drops cracking like pistol shots on the shingles of the awning, and he turned and hurried after his boss as the rancher moved towards the private gambling rooms at the back of the big bar, casually acknowledging all the greetings from drinkers as he did so. It wasn't popularity, though. Nor respect. More like something that had to be done – or better be done. . . .

Lee Fargo was leaning against the clapboards of the general store under the awning, enjoying watching the clouds swirl and roll in the sky, back-lit by lightning, apparently kicked across space by the following explosion of thunder.

Quite a storm coming, he allowed silently as he twisted up his cigarette, placed it between his lips and fumbled in a shirt pocket for a vesta. But he didn't light the smoke right away, paused to watch the young woman walking along the boardwalk opposite, heading towards the lighted front of the town's posh hotel, the Rockwell Arms. Yeah – a big storm coming. Maybe bigger than some folk expected. . . .

The girl stepped down from the walk to cross the badly lighted side street, head down, holding on to her hat as the wind flattened her clothes against her lithe young body. Fargo snapped his match into life, blinding himself for a moment, as he dipped the end of the cigarette into the flame.

When he looked up, simultaneously shaking out the vesta and blowing the first lungful of smoke with the cigarette still in his mouth, he saw that the girl had disappeared. She hadn't had time to cross the street

and reach the entrance to the hotel . . . and she would-
n't go down the shadowy, narrow street to the side
entrance.

He stiffened when he heard a quickly stifled scream
from the darkness over there. He flicked away his cigarette and started to run across Main. Some of the other
loungers looked up from whatever they were doing,
watching him sprint through the first raindrops of the
storm. Lightning blazed and thunder crashed as he
skidded into the mouth of the narrow side street. He
glimpsed struggling figures, a woman being jostled
against a wall of the hotel by a man. A couple of the
men stood up, hesitated, then started across as Fargo
ran into the street, making for the grappling forms.

The man had a hand over the girl's mouth, but Fargo
could hear her muffled cries and then the attacker
yelled as her teeth sank into his flesh and he wrenched
his hand away and slapped her hard.

'Get away from her!' snapped Fargo, reaching for
the man, feeling cloth tear under his grip as he spun
the attacker towards him.

He glimpsed a rain-wet, stubbled face and wild eyes,
bared teeth. Then his arm was smashed aside and the
man swung at Fargo's head. The young cowboy weaved
aside and planted a blow into the man's midriff,
doubling him up. He lifted a knee into the contorted
face and the man slammed back against the wet clapboards, head rapping the timber. The attacker staggered, dazed, and Fargo moved in, hammering blows
into his hard body, jarring him violently. The man
swung wildly, connected twice, but there was little sting

in the blows. Fargo's left put him down on one knee and then there were yells and pounding footsteps behind him as other men ran into the street. Fargo hauled the dazed attacker to his feet by his shirt front, shoved him away violently.

'Get out of here before I pound your face into dog meat!' he gritted, and the man staggered away into the blackness.

Someone yelled, '*Hey*!' and Fargo turned, stumbling – right into the path of two men who were obviously going to give chase to the fleeing man. They went down in a tangle, the earth of the street now churned to mud with the rain, and they were a mess when they stood up, clawing at each other for balance.

By then the fugitive had gone: they couldn't even hear his running footsteps over the hammering of the rain.

'Damn!' one man said, looking hard at Fargo. 'We coulda caught and held the sonuver!'

'Forget him – we better see to the girl,' Fargo said, turning.

She was cowering against the wall, holding her torn bodice close, pale and frightened, blinking as lightning seared the alleyway. She cringed away from Fargo's reaching hand and he dropped it back to his side.

'You all right, miss?'

She stared and then nodded and one of the townsmen – there was a tight group of rubbernecks gathering at the entrance to the street by now – said, 'Holy Pete! That's the Rockwell gal!'

Fargo turned, frowning, looking puzzled. Then the

onlookers scattered as Rip Ohlrig came smashing through, pushing and shoving, clearing a way for Kent Rockwell. The big rancher went straight to the girl, held her close and she clung to him. He looked at Ohlrig.

'Get this place cleared! Come on! Get the hell outa the way! Let me through!'

Half-carrying the upset girl, her feet barely touching the puddles and mud, Rockwell moved through the crowd as Ohlrig opened a way for him.

Lee Fargo skirted the jostling men and went back towards Main, on the opposite side of the narrow street to Rockwell and the girl. Running through the rain, he headed for the batwings of the Lone Star, drenched now, feeling the need for a whiskey with a beer chaser . . .

He had had two by the time he became aware of the buzz of conversation in the bar dying around him. As he started to turn, he bumped into the tall man who had battered a way through the crowd in the side street so roughly. Water dripped from the curlbrim hat and part of his face was in shadow. Narrow like an axe blade, and with about as much warmth, Fargo told himself as hard, bitter eyes looked him over. His clothes were muddy from the side street but beneath the soiling it was clear to see they were a working-man's shirt and Levis. Rip Ohlrig's gaze lingered briefly on the gunbelt and holstered sixgun, noted the rawhide thong holding the base of the holster to Fargo's thigh, and the little loop that hooked over the hammer, assuring the gun stayed in place.

'You got a name, feller?'

Fargo met the man's stare, finished the last of his beer before replying, 'Fargo.'

'Kin of Wells, Fargo, no doubt.'

'Sorry to say I'm not. Who're you?'

There was a hissing of indrawn breath from close-by drinkers but the lean man said evenly enough, 'Rip Ohlrig.'

Like the name ought to mean something to Fargo.

The cowboy continued to stare back, face blank. 'What can I do for you?'

'Stranger, ain't you?' Ohlrig asked, ignoring the question.

'Rode in around sundown. Saw the storm a'brewing and figured to find me a dry bed for the night.' Fargo spread his hands, indicating his muddy clothes. 'Almost made it.'

Ohlrig didn't crack a smile, continued to look him over. He saw a man only an inch or so shorter than his own six feet one, young – early twenties, maybe – deep-tanned like a rifle butt, whip-lean but there was enough movement in the drinking arm to tell Ohlrig this hombre was pretty fit.

'What're you doin' here?'

'Having a drink – or was, until you showed up.'

'I'll buy you a drink.' Ohlrig nodded to the hovering barkeep who drew another glass of beer and set it on the counter at Fargo's elbow.

The young cowboy made no move to touch the glass. 'Why?' When Ohlrig frowned, he added, 'Why buy me a drink?'

'Reward – fot rescuin' Miss Liza from that scum.'

Fargo arched his eyebrows. 'Liza? That her name? No trouble – smelled likker on the man. He seemed half-hearted about it all.'

Ohlrig snorted. 'Tell that to Miss Liza! She's badly shook-up.'

'Sorry to hear it – I got there as fast as I could when I heard her scream.'

'You did all right. C'mon, drink your beer. Her father wants to see you.'

Lee Fargo appeared to stiffen slightly, paused with the drink a few inches above the counter top. 'Kent Rockwell?'

Ohlrig's eyes narrowed and there was a subtle shifting of shoulder muscles under his wet shirt. 'You know him?'

'Hell no. Someone said it was the Rockwell girl and everyone's heard of the Rocking R and this town they say is practically owned by Rockwell.'

'*Mr Rockwell* . . . he don't like to be kept waitin'.'

Fargo shrugged, downed his beer, wiped a hand across his lips and hitched his gunbelt. He was amused to see Ohlrig take a wary step backward, his own hand moving closer to his gun butt. 'Ready when you are.'

Rockwell occupied half the top floor of the hotel. There were so many rooms it reminded Fargo of a small house. He felt conspicuous and a mite embarrassed as he stood there in his wet, muddy clothes, dripping on to the expensive-looking carpet, hat in his hands, thick dark-brown hair flattened to his skull from the battered crown.

Kent Rockwell had shaken his hand, said little, now stood back looking him over while Ohlrig poured a couple of brandies into large, balloon-type glasses. He handed one to Fargo and the other to Rockwell, deadpan. He did not take a drink himself, but stood by the small ornately carved bar, hips leaning against the dark wood, watching.

'As we say here in Texas, *muchas gracias, amigo*. You saved my daughter from what could've been a mighty nasty situation.'

'Glad I happened along.' Fargo took a gulp of brandy and felt the fumes rising behind his eyes, but it slid down his throat like velvet. 'Mighty fine likker, Mr Rockwell.'

'Better sipped than gulped,' the rancher said curtly. '*Happened* along, you say – is that right?'

Fargo frowned. 'Yeah, it's right. I was outside the general store, had just bought a sack of tobacco, papers and vestas, when I saw the girl hurrying along the other side of the street.'

'My daughter.'

'I didn't know who she was. I lit my quirly and when I looked up she'd gone – but I heard a muffled scream coming from the side street and ran across. . . .'

The young cowboy straightened an inch or so as Rockwell continued to stare at him, walking around him now. Rip Ohlrig didn't move a muscle, his gaze drilling into Fargo.

'You a drifter, son?' Rockwell asked.

'I'm drifting between jobs, is all,' Fargo said stiffly. 'I'm riding grubline, but only because I haven't found work yet.'

'So you came to this town,' Ohlrig said, somehow making it sound like a wrong move.

'Yeah – I heard down-trail that there might be work in Rockwell County, and as Santa Laga is the county seat. . . .' He shrugged, then set his gaze squarely on Kent Rockwell's face. 'Why? You offering me a job?'

Ohlrig straightened but Fargo didn't look towards him. Kent's eyes narrowed.

'That what you want me to do?'

Fargo heaved a sigh. 'Look, Mr Rockwell, I dunno what's going on here – I figured when this feller told me you wanted to see me, that you wanted to thank me for what I did. There's no need, but, like I said, I'm riding grubline, and if there was a chance of a few bucks or the offer of a job, I reckoned I'd better come along.'

Ohlrig was closer now and jostled Fargo. 'You'd've come anyway.'

Fargo looked at him. 'Only if I'd wanted to.'

'You'd've come.' Flat. Never a doubt about it.

Kent watched the two men striking sparks from each other.

Then a door opened and Liza Rockwell came in. She wore a gown that went all the way to the floor, brushing pink slippers. She was pale, her face pinched and nervous. Then she smiled tentatively and came up to Fargo, offering him a small hand almost shyly. He took it gingerly.

'I owe you my life, Mr Fargo.' She sounded shaky, though her voice was warm, too.

'I dunno about that, but I hope you're feeling better, miss.'

'Thank you.' She turned to her father, Ohlrig hovering: he looked as if he wanted to hurry the girl out of here. 'Father, I heard Mr Fargo say he came here looking for work – surely we can find him a job on Rocking R?'

'Look, miss,' Fargo began, but Rockwell held up a hand, his gaze still on the young man's face.

'Your clothes say you're a cowpoke, but what've you done? Where are you from?'

'Listen, it doesn't matter.' Fargo started to turn away. 'I dunno what all the fuss is about, but I'll find work or I won't and I'll move on. . . .' He nodded to Liza as he put on his hat. 'Glad I could help out, miss. Thanks for the drink, Mr Rockwell.'

His hand reached for the door-knob but suddenly Rip Ohlrig was blocking his path. 'Mr Rockwell will tell you when you can leave.'

Fargo took his time looking over his shoulder towards the rancher. The girl stood tensed, hands clasped in front of her, mouth slightly open.

'Come back here, son,' the rancher said abruptly. 'I can find you a job – and you'll stay here in this hotel tonight as my guest. We'll head out to the ranch tomorrow.'

Liza smiled and Fargo thought the whole room seemed brighter.

He was given a room on the floor below the Rockwell suite, complete with bath which a Mexican kid filled with hot water and where he soaked some of the trail aches and dirt from his lean frame. Rockwell even sent down a set of new clothes, complete with spare shirt.

He pulled on the stiff new Levis and, barefoot and bare-chested, sat on the edge of the soft mattress and rolled a cigarette. He was about to light it when there was a quiet rapping sound – at the balcony window.

Fargo casually picked up his Colt and padded across, pulling aside the brown-paper blind a little. A face that could have been made out of weathered leather, framed by long silver hair beneath a ragged old army slouch hat, stared back at him, rheumy eyes squinting.

Fargo opened the blind about halfway and lifted the window. A wave of animal-like odour reached his nostrils, but he did not recoil. The bearded lips peeled back from chipped and missing teeth.

'You do smell fine, ma'am!'

Fargo grinned tightly. 'Too bad I can't say the same for you.'

'Put me alongside a grizz and he'd slip an arm around me – put you there and he'd rip you apart.'

Lee Fargo laughed quietly, looking out both ways along the narrow veranda. 'You coming in?'

'Better if I don't . . . I take it you ain't payin' for this room, or them new Levis?'

'Gifts from a grateful father.'

'Then it – worked?'

'Like a charm. We ride for Rocking R tomorrow. I'm the new wrangler.'

Sam'l Houston Noble grinned wider, punched Fargo lightly on the bare chest.

'Now ain't all this better'n an Injun tipi stinkin' of smoke an' piss an' rancid hides?'

He was surprised when Fargo said quite seriously, 'I'll let you know, Sam – I'll let you know.'

3
Blackmail

Rip Ohlrig's face was harder than usual as he entered Kent Rockwell's rooms in the hotel. The rancher was breakfasting at a table by the window and looked up.

'Eaten?'

'Earlier. Listen, boss, I've just been talking with Liza and—'

He broke off as Rockwell's face straightened and his eyes became like chips of flint. 'She's supposed to be resting, goddamnit! She's not to be disturbed this early!'

Ohlrig held up a hand. 'I saw her on her balcony from my room and she waved and I called could I come up and—'

'Well?' the rancher snapped.

'She's recovering OK, a lot better this morning, so I asked her a few questions about the attack.'

The rancher started to get up, face like a thunderhead rising over a mountain range, but once again Rip

29

held up a placating hand, forestalling the angry rancher.

'She said she was up to it and she recognized the son of a bitch who jumped her.' Rip got this last out with a rush so as to head off any more interruptions by Rockwell.

The rancher paused in his forward movement, sat down again and picked up his cup of coffee, watching his foreman over the rim as he drank.

'She thinks it was Gabe Luckett.'

'*That* miserable scum? But – *thinks*?'

'Not too sure and you can't blame her, comin' at her out of the dark like that, but she's pretty sure that's who it was.'

'He's dirt all the way through to his backbone, is Gabe Luckett, like all the damn Lucketts – but I thought he'd have more sense than to try somethin' with a daughter of mine.'

'Liza says he reeked of booze.'

'Well, that could explain it, I suppose. You'd better get some of the boys looking for him.'

'Already have, been through the town twice and I've had a couple of looksees myself. He ain't in town, boss. Which sort of makes it look as if Liza was right. He'd hightail it for sure.'

Rockwell lifted one arm, index finger rigid. 'Find him: put a bounty on the bastard. I want him brought in to me. Savvy? Beat the hell outa him, kick his butt clear across the Brazos, but make sure he's still breathin' when you dump him at my feet. You got it?'

Ohlrig nodded. 'It'll be done, boss. One other thing: this kid, Fargo. . . .'

'What about him?'

'You told him he could be wrangler, but Mickey's miffed, says it's been his job for nigh on twenty years an' he ain't had no complaints from you.'

'The hell with how Mickey feels – but you can tell him Fargo'll be his sidekick for a spell. He's not losing his job.'

'OK.' Ohlrig started to turn away, hesitated, then faced the rancher once more. 'You recall an old buff'lo hunter or mountain man with long silver hair, wears mostly buckskins, stinks like a polecat?'

Rip was surprised at the way Rockwell's head snapped around and the man's cup clattered noisily as he replaced it in his saucer. His voice was harsh as he said, 'Used to be a feller named Noble looked like that. Did a little work for Rockin' R long ago when he'd had a bad season. Before your time.'

'Didn't know that, but I've seen him around a few times . . . includin' last night. Right here.'

Rockwell was obviously tensed now. 'What d'you mean *here*? In the hotel?'

'Yeah, well, leavin' it. Spotted him comin' down the outside stairway from the second floor. Where Fargo's room is.'

Rockwell had gone very still. 'What's that mean?'

'I dunno – just a hunch I guess.'

'You don't like me taking on Fargo, do you?'

Rip shrugged. 'Not for me to say – but I figured it was a bit – lucky – that he just happened to be around when Luckett jumped Liza, when he was hard up for a job.'

'By Christ, you better be wrong there!'

'Well, I asked around. There was one feller, the old soak they call Brandy, says he seen Fargo buyin' Luckett a drink in the bar of the Lonesome Gal.'

'That dump!'

'Well, it's the kinda place Brandy hangs out, but not where you'd expect to find Fargo.'

'Brandy'd say whatever he thought you wanted him to if it meant a free drink.'

'Yeah, well, I bought him a couple, I admit, but it's worth rememberin', boss. There's somethin' about that kid that don't seem quite right. There's some sort of accent there.'

'Keep an eye on him then, but get Gabe Luckett fast.'

Ohlrig left and Rockwell sat at the table, coffee growing cold, as he stared out of the window, seeing nothing of what was happening in the street below.

He was thinking back twenty years to a buckskin-clad buffalo hunter who looked old beyond his years and had shoulder-length silver hair even then.

He'd thought the son of a bitch had died years ago.

Gabe Luckett made it through the storm as far as the small town of Spur during the night. He was a mess when he arrived at his brother's shack on the outskirts of town and dried out in front of the fire.

'You make yourself Java if you want,' growled Rance, the elder of the Lucketts. 'I'm goin' back to bed so don't make a racket.'

Gabe shivered, holding a threadbare blanket about

his shoulders. He sniffled and wiped his hair with one edge of the blanket.

'You won't be so snotty when I show you what I got.'

Rance, settling in his smelly bed, paused with the grimy blanket pulled almost to his chin. 'Yeah? You got booze. . . ?'

'No, I—'

'Then I ain't interested. Now shut up and lemme sleep.'

'Aaah, I dunno why you're always such a damn grouch.'

Gabe settled on a tree-stump seat near the fire, muttering to himself as the blanket began to steam. He tossed another piece of firewood on and looked towards his brother's bunk. The man was snoring, his wiry black beard quivering with each breath. Gabe curled a lip, but he couldn't hold himself back. He went to his saddle-bags near his pile of wet clothes, rummaged deep and walked over to stand beside Rance's bed. Grinning tightly, he held up the chamois bag by its rawhide drawstring and let it fall on Rance's chest.

The elder Luckett roared as he jerked upright, eyes flying wide, staring wildly around him – then heard the clink of coins as the drawstring poke rolled down his blanket-covered body. It had his instant attention and he held it up, shaking it again to make it clink. He snapped his gaze towards his grinning younger brother.

Narrowing his reddened eyes, he opened the bag and peeked in, turning it a little to catch the firelight. 'Judas priest! Gold! Where the hell'd you get this? Aw, now, listen, if you've slit some drunk's throat in Santa Laga you ain't gonna hide out here!'

'Relax,' said Gabe, snatching the poke away from Rance who didn't like that much but he continued to glare, awaiting an explanation. 'I earned this – real easy, too. All I had to do was make out I was attackin' a young gal and let this feller come to her "rescue", punch me a coupla times before kickin' my ass and sendin' me on my way.' He shook the bag and the coins clinked. 'Him and his pard paid all this just for that!'

Rance didn't believe him, he could see that, but he repeated the story and insisted it was true. 'Hell, who was it you had to attack? The Queen of England!'

'Nah – you can disbelieve me all you want, but I'm here to tell you it's gospel. All I had to do was let this young feller be a hero and his old pard gave me this poke of gold. . . . Hell, the gal only got her blouse ripped, not hurt at all.'

Rance frowned deeper. 'Who was it?'

'Feller name of Lee Fargo and his pard was Sam Noble, a mountain man or somethin'.'

'Heard of Noble, but he was s'posed to've been killed by Injuns years ago – but I meant, who was the gal?'

'Rancher's daughter.' Gabe mumbled it and his gaze was suddenly shifty. Rance sat up straighter in bed.

'Who – was – it? Damn you, Gabe, you come clean with me, boy, or I'll flay the hide off you till I see your backbone!'

Gabe had had a taste of Brother Rance's bullwhip a couple of times in the past and he had no notion to try for a third. He took a deep breath. 'Liza Rockwell.'

Rance's lantern jaw sagged. He couldn't speak for a long moment. When he did his voice was no more than a hoarse whisper. 'Tell me you're jokin'! *Pl-eeease* tell me you're joshin' me!'

Gabe swallowed, shook his head, then rattled the poke again. 'Like I said, she weren't hurt none. She never seen me in that dark side street. It was too good to pass up, Rance! A hundred bucks just for mussin' her hair a little.'

Rance swung his hairy legs over the side of the bed. 'Why'd this Fargo want to make her think he was a hero? He taken a shine to her?'

'Dunno. I think he wanted a job on Rockin' R and seen this as a way of gettin' one.'

'Why the hell would he go to all that trouble just to get a forty-an'-found job punchin' cows? Hell, there's a dozen ranches over there'd take him on just by askin'. . . .'

'No, it had to be Rockwell. Heard him an' Noble talkin' . . . they cooked it up between 'em.'

'Then they got some deal goin'! That Sam Noble, he was mixed up in a lot of shady stuff years ago – sellin' gurls to the Injuns, jumpin' other buff'lo runners and stealin' their hides. Like I said, word was he got killed. Apaches I think it was s'posed to be. If he's back with this kid an' they set up that deal, you can bet there's a lot more'n a hundred bucks to be made.'

Gabe felt something clutch at his belly, like a closing fist deep down. He might have known Brother Rance would buy into this somehow! He was the smart one, but, *hell!* This was meant to be Gabe's own deal! Now Rance was thinking deeply and that sly smile was showing and Gabe just knew he was going to take over. . . .

Rance suddenly smiled, threw an arm around Gabe's shoulders. 'Bro', let's you an' me get some sleep and we'll head into town soon as the saloon's open in the mornin' and by then I'll have it all sorted out in my mind.'

'Have what sorted out? Judas, Rance, I don't want no complications! I done the job and I'm happy with what I been paid.'

Rance tightened his grip on Gabe's shoulders and shook him. 'Gabe, a hundred bucks is only spit compared to what we can make outa this!'

'But there ain't anythin' else! Fargo just wanted the job and my guess is he got it . . . that's all there is to it.'

'Don't believe so, Bro'. If he'd pay you a hundred bucks just for mussin'-up Liza Rockwell, he's hopin' to make a heap more.'

'Well, mebbe he is, but we can't wait around—'

'Don't have to! How much you reckon he'll pay us to keep our mouths shut?' Gabe blinked and Rance smirked. 'Yeah, little brother, you don't think things all the way through, never have! But I can see we're gonna be rich men without hardly havin' to do anythin' more'n hint that we might let slip to Rockwell how Fargo set himself up as a "heero"! C'mon, Gabe, let's get some shut-eye so's we'll be fresh come mornin'. You can dream of all that money we're gonna be makin'!'

Gabe would like it to be true but he had never yet known one of Rance's get-rich-quick schemes to work out.

4

The Bronco-Buster

The whole ground trembled. Thunder came up from over the rise, its source only vaguely marked by the swirling dust which tailed out behind the running mustangs.

Riders yelled and cussed, waved hats, slapped at dusty hides, taking desperate chances as they spurred their mounts in, kicked some of the rolling-eyed mustangs in the direction they wished them to go. More than one had to rein sharply aside in order to miss the snapping teeth or the bumping shoulder.

These horses had been free for a long time and had no notion to be herded into corrals.

There were ten riders and Lee Fargo was in the lead. Mickey Gann, the wrangler, rode hard and expertly up in the front, too, but some of his attention was directed to Fargo and not all given to the team of horses. He hadn't been impressed by Rockwell's assurance that he,

Gann, would still remain head wrangler. He knew what a tough-minded sonuver Kent Rockwell was – and if he figured Fargo was the better man, then it was Fargo who would end up with the job.

And, goddamnit! Fargo was good!

Maybe the best rider Mickey Gann had ever seen and that was saying plenty. Gann had busted broncs for the army, ridden in rodeos, could sit astride a horse before he could walk. He had seen 'em all and Lee Fargo was up there with the best. Reminded him of a Comanche brave the way he sat big and square in the saddle, elbows tucked in against his hips, using the reins with minimal movements, knees and heels sending signals to the racing horse. Comanches were held as being the best horsemen anywhere so it was quite a compliment for Gann to even think that Fargo was as good as any of them he had seen.

Not only that, the young wrangler knew horses like a preacher knew his psalms. He could almost talk to them – *and* nearly get a damn response! Why, Gann had seen a horse being spoken to and gentled by Fargo literally place its head on his shoulder and look for a goddamn cuddle! Yeah! He'd actually seen that and told himself it had never happened. But he knew better.

And the thing Kent Rockwell was going to like best of all about this Fargo was the way he trapped the horses. It was nothing new to rig an alleyway for wild horses, leading them to where the corrals waited, using existing trees, or stakes driven into the ground where necessary, stringing lengths of burlap between them. The running horses just saw a wall coming up, couldn't see beyond, so veered the way the wall went, racing alongside, looking for an opening – and ending up in the corrals, trying to kick the rails to splinters in their frustration.

Mickey Gann had used the method for years, but when you were working the same country year after year, the wise old lead stallion soon became used to it and made a run at the flimsy walls, tearing through and leading his mares and colts after him with ragged streamers of burlap left flapping in the breeze.

But Fargo had fixed that – just under the top of the burlap where it was usually rolled over rope to hold it up, he strung a length of barbed wire. A couple of runs at that and with his fresh wounds streaming blood, the lead stallion shrilled in protest and, knowing there was no other way to go, turned to follow the path of the twin walls of burlap, aware of where it would lead but having no choice. . . .

Because of this, they had considerably cut their losses of escaping mustangs and would fill the corrals twice over in half the time. When Rockwell knew *that*, Lee Fargo was going to be well on the way to becoming the new wrangler.

Mickey Gann swore bitterly as he saw the plan was working. OK, the big black stallion was streaming blood on his chest and withers but they had never managed to hold him, anyway. He always found some way out and had never had bridle or even a sackcloth blindfold on him. So he would leap the corral fence again this time – the only one big and strong enough to do it – and they would lose him as usual, but they would have more horses to be broken in than they had at any other round-up.

Gann could *spit!* He glared through the dust at Fargo, standing in his stirrups now, guiding his sweating chestnut by twitches of his leg muscles and murmured commands. He twirled his rope, legs flexing with the movement of the big chestnut as it weaved this way and that, bottling up the spotted horse Fargo was after, so that all he had to do was practically lean over and drop the rope loop over its head. It might gall Gann to see it done, but he was honest enough to admire the skill and horsemanship of the young rider.

'You've trained that chestnut well,' he called.

Fargo grinned through the mask of dust on his face, effortlessly pulling the spotted horse towards him. 'We work good together. I get along OK with horses.'

'Christ, better than OK!'

Fargo seemed pleased and continued with the work of cutting out the next horse selected for breaking-in. Maybe that was where he would fall down thought Mickey. Literally!

He was wrong. Fargo rode the mustang to a standstill in an afternoon and had it following him around the corral while he shook out his rope, ready to lasso his next animal. Funny how the spooked horses in the working corrals seemed to calm down when he appeared. . . .

Another thing, Gann thought to himself irritably. Gann himself was mighty glad to see the end of a day of busting mule-headed broncs, grunted and creaked his way to supper, shovelled in his food and gulped his hot

coffee and limped away to his bedroll, sleeping the
sleep of the dead. Fargo? Hell, the son of a bitch made
his way around the camp in the hills, playing a hand of
cards here, helping another ranny plait a quirt there,
lending a hand to a cowboy trying to patch a hole in the
sole of his boots. And then he'd go for a walk along the
goddamn creek!

Mickey groaned in his blankets. Hell, he wasn't that
old! Or was it just that Fargo was that *young*, full of sap
and energy Mickey Gann had had battered out of him
over years of horse-breaking. . . . Ah, the hell with it! He
needed his sleep, *needed* it!

So he tilted his hat over his eyes and was soon snoring while Fargo made his way along the creek-bank
until he was hidden from the camp by live oaks and a
heavy patch of mesquite. Then he turned upslope into
the trees, climbed almost to the top of the rise until he
saw the movement of a shadow against the stars.

He smelled Sam'l Houston Noble from ten yards
away, downslope and with the wind at his back.

The old man's silver hair gleamed in the light of the
half moon and although his face was shaded by the
battered brim of the old army hat he wore these days,
Fargo thought he saw the flash of teeth in a welcoming
smile.

'You ain't forgot your Injun ways with hosses, I see,'
greeted Noble.

'You been watching the round-up? Gann sends riders
all over, so you better be careful.'

'They won't see me 'less I want 'em to see me. You havin' trouble with Gann?'

'No-oo – but he doesn't like my being there much. Ohlrig seems to have some sort of chip on his shoulder, too.'

'That's his way – everyone's a pain in the butt far as he's concerned 'cept for Kent Rockwell and *he's* the only one you gotta really worry about. If he's happy with you, then everyone else *has* to be the same or draw their time. How's the gal?'

Fargo sobered. 'Sent back to her school wherever that is – but she's still kinda jumpy. That damn Luckett went for her like he meant it, the sonuver!'

'That's what we paid him for, boy,' Noble said quietly. 'Had to be realistic.'

'I know, but – well, she's so damn young. Innocent.'

'Not as young or as innocent as you when you were s'posed to be left to die in the wilds.'

Fargo was silent, then nodded jerkily. 'Don't recollect much about that. Fact, Sam, all I recollect is what you've told me.'

'Sure. The mind's a funny thing – just won't remember what it don't want to if it's bad. Sawbones from Boston told me that one time when I guided him an' his party into the Palo Duro to shoot buff. He was the only one wanted to do the whole thing himself, the stalkin', loadin' his shells, sightin'-in his rifle – the others had me do it all while they stayed in camp drinkin' and playin' cards. 'Course they went home with their buffalo hides and plenty of wild stories to make 'em out heroes, but that sawbones, he wanted to do the lot, even down to helpin' with the skinnin'. . . .'

'Sam, I better not stay away too long. Things are going OK. Give me time to win Rockwell's confidence and find out what's happening. You'd best stay away for a spell. S'pose I meet you a week from tonight?'

'Too damn long! I want to know what's happenin' long before that. You ask questions: they'll savvy you wantin' to know things, you bein' young and new to Rockin' R. You'll learn just as much by the questions they tell you ain't none of your business, the touchy ones. . . .'

Fargo nodded. 'I know what to do.'

'Figured you'd be more enthusiastic, boy!'

'Sam, we've been together for nigh on seven years, since you snatched me away from the tribe and told me who I am. I've worked with you and we've found out a lot. I'm just not sure that I need to be down there on Rocking R now.'

'Well, you sure ain't got enough money to call in the lawyers, so we gotta do it this way.' Noble's voice was curt and edgy and Fargo looked hard at him, straining to see the expression on that shadowed face.

'You owe Rockwell something, don't you?'

Noble was silent for a short time. 'I do,' he said finally. He hadn't talked so much in years until he'd found this boy. Now it seemed there were times he couldn't shut up – even when he ought to. 'He messed up my whole damn life! Let me think he was hidin' me out and all the time I didn't need him, I was a free man and he let me go on thinkin' I had the law after me. I lost the only gal I ever loved, boy, a daughter, too. All because Rockwell

seen a way to use me. . . .' He snorted. 'Hell, I paved the
way for the likes of Rip Ohlrig and all the other guns he
hired before him . . . but you never mind about what *I*
owe Rockwell; you just keep thinkin' about what he owes
you.'

'Yeah, OK. Sam, I get a notion that I'm kind of a
disappointment to you. That I'm not the – savage – you
hoped or figured I was.'

Noble cackled. 'You got a good brain on you, boy.
That's what counts. Lookit the way you come up with a
name in that town in Mississippi. You seen the picture
of good ol' Robert E. Lee on the courthouse wall, and
the Wells, Fargo depot across the way . . . two shakes an'
you said you'd call yourself "Lee Fargo". You think
quick, son, and you think smart. No, I ain't disap-
pointed in you. You're gonna go all the way with this
and I'm gonna be right alongside you when you stand
there and tell that bastard Kent Rockwell just who you
are and what you want from him!'

Rockwell was reading a *Cattlemen's Association Bulletin*,
sitting up in bed, when there was a knock on the door
of his room. He looked up irritably and swung his gaze
to the old wooden-framed clock on the timber walls set
amongst a couple of deer and mountain-lion heads.
Almost ten o'clock!

'Who the hell is it at this time of night?' he called.

The door partly opened and Ohlrig's head and
shoulders appeared. He didn't speak. Rockwell jerked
his head for him to enter and saw the lanky ramrod was
carrying what looked like a soft buckskin envelope. He

glanced up at Rip's unsmiling face as the man stopped beside the bed and held the buckskin out towards him.

Rockwell made no move to take the package. 'You got Gabe Luckett yet?'

Rip shook his head. 'Got men lookin'. We know he went to brother Rance's place in Spur but they've both disappeared.'

Rockwell snorted. 'Check out the saloons within a hundred-mile radius! That's where you'll find them two.'

Ohlrig nodded, thrust the buckskin towards the rancher again. 'We'll get 'em, boss. Here – figured it was a good time to go through Fargo's warbag while he's out on the range. Had to wait till the others were asleep.'

Still watching Ohlrig's face, Rockwell took the envelope, felt something almost insubstantial inside, one end of which was weighed down by some round item, its shape showing through the soft buckskin. He noticed now that it was painted with Indian-style decorations – stick-like figures indicating animals and men, some diamond shapes, one inside the other, half-circles with dots over and under the line.

'Comanche,' he murmured, and pulled out the flap of the envelope. There was an eagle feather inside, a little worn and frayed but still beautiful. He held it up, twirled it between thumb and finger by the spine. 'Injuns figure this as the ultimate sign of good medicine.' He set it down, took out a folded strip of rawhide, also decorated. He frowned as he held it by the ends, scanning the painting. 'Headband. Something about a big wolf – no, not big – *tall* – a tall wolf with a – a white coat?'

Rockwell flicked his gaze up to Rip Ohlrig's face and it seemed to the ramrod that his boss was suddenly a mite paler and more tense, but his voice gave nothing away when he spoke.'You ever seen a white wolf?'

'No, but I hear they're around.'

Rockwell seemed as if he would say more but then his probing fingers touched the cold round metal of the item in the bottom of the envelope. He fumbled in his hurry to get it out and – *By God!* – Rip knew he wasn't mistaken this time! Rockwell's face *had* lost a deal of colour as he looked down at the coin now lying in the palm of his hand.

It had a hole punched through the middle and a smaller one near the rim. The date was 1861.

'My guess is the feather was fixed to that and some-one wore it as protection against the bad spirits.' There was contempt in Rip's voice but Rockwell didn't look up. 'Somethin' scratched into the back.'

He examined the coin closely, seemed reluctant to turn it over. Then he did and Ohlrig heard the sharp indrawing of the rancher's breath as he ran a shaking finger over the design cut deeply into the soft silver.

An *R* resting on a short arc of a circle.

'Damn if that don't look just like the Rockin' R brand, boss – don't it?'

5

Loner

Rip Ohlrig was no fool: he saw how good Fargo was with horses and he knew Mickey Gann resented the young cowboy's expertise. Anyone else and Ohlrig might have been tempted to fire Gann and replace him with Fargo as head wrangler.

But there was something about that kid that bothered him. The Indian items, and, in particular, that coin, had upset Kent Rockwell considerably although he hadn't explained why to Ohlrig. That was OK, though: Rip was used to Rockwell's moods and not being told things that didn't really concern him. Only thing was, he had a nagging hunch that this time it did – or would – concern him. He wished he knew what it was about Fargo that burned him the way it did just seeing the man. . . .

'Fargo!' he called, as the sweating bronc-buster climbed down off yet another mustang he had broken-in to the saddle.

Fargo wiped sweat and dirt from his face with a neckerchief as he sauntered across, still a little breathless from the pounding he had taken atop the horse.

'See that draw yonder? Way over near the base of that sawtooth ridge?' Ohlrig said without pointing. 'You just won yourself the job of clearin' the timber out of there. Want it done by week's end. Gives you three days. Ride back to the ranch and ask the blacksmith for axes and saws.' He turned away without waiting for a response and Fargo stared after him without expression. That was one of the things that riled Ohlrig, the foreman allowed, as he glanced over his shoulder: the son of a bitch did what he was told all right but you could never tell how he took it – his face was unreadable. Like a damn Injun's!

There was a lot of timber to be cleared – live oaks, pecan, water elm, ash, hickory and gum. Spanish moss hung from the branches like elongated scalps. And there was chaparral and mesquite with a patch of sotol thrown in. The roots seemed to deliberately entangle his feet and twice he almost snapped his ankle, saved only by the good leather of the high uppers of his riding boots. No one came to help him and after the first night of having to prepare his own supper at the end of a day's work – which did not end until full dark – he decided he needed plenty of food when working like this and that jerky or cold biscuits didn't give enough nourishment, not even with the molasses Cooky had given him.

Sam Noble had taught him to be self-sufficient in

the mountain-man way, so he rode into the ranch and borrowed a Dutch oven from the one-legged cook. He shot a couple of jack-rabbits while the early morning mists were still in the draw, skinned and gutted them, cut up some carrots and potatoes and onions, and tossed in a handful of beans and sage and wild herbs for flavour. With salt and water, he buried the pot under hot coals from his camp-fire and set it a'cooking. Come sundown, he uncovered it and it was still hot and savoury and made a good nourishing stew that fed back some of the energy he had expended during the day.

He didn't make Ohlrig's deadline, but he knew the ramrod hadn't expected him to, had only used 'the short time-limit to put pressure on him. But Ohlrig rode in and looked at the trees that had been felled and the brush that had been cleared, plainly surprised so much had been accomplished.

'Need to strip them branches off them tree-trunks and have the rest of the draw cleared by the time I get back.'

'Get back?'

'That's what I said. If it ain't done when I come out next time to check, you're through here, and even the boss won't argue about that.'

Fargo merely nodded and Ohlrig swore under his breath. That damned stoical acceptance was beginning to scald him!

'Get it done!' he snapped as he wheeled his horse and spurred away.

That night Noble came to the shadows just beyond

the circle of light cast by Fargo's camp-fire.

'See the sonuver's bustin' your back for you. Was tempted to come on down and lend a hand but figured I might be seen.'

'I'll manage – but he sure does have it in for me.'

He dished out some of the rabbit stew and casually pushed it behind the log he was sitting on. He didn't think anyone from Rocking R was spying on him but he figured to play it safe. He heard Noble take the tin bowl and spoon but didn't actually see him do it.

'Right tasty. Needs a mite more salt is all. They're keepin' you away from the ranch. Gonna make it hard for you to get a look in Rockwell's desk.'

'Thought of giving myself a cut with the axe, not too bad, but bad enough to have me ride in for help and hang around the bunkhouse for a day or two.'

'Might work – but you be careful. You don't want to cripple yourself or bleed to death.'

'I can make it look good. There's plenty of wild medicine around here I can use to heal it quick, but they won't know that and I can drag it out some. . . .'

'We-ell – you be careful. We need a look at his papers but don't take chances. If you're caught that's the end of the whole she-bang.'

'Cooky said Ohlrig's kept a couple of hardcases on the spread, ready to ride at a minute's notice. They're looking for someone and I think it's Gabe Luckett.'

The spoon clattered on the tin bowl. 'Damn! Hell, he'll've been boozin' away that money we give him, likely with his brother, Rance, a real mean snake. Gabe can't go long without his booze. If they get their hands on him while he's sweatin' bullets, lookin' for his next drink, he's gonna talk.'

'Thought we agreed he'd clear the Brazos and stay away?'

Noble snorted. 'Gabe'd agree to anythin' that'd put him next to a bottle of redeye, but when that bottle's gone, he'll do whatever he has to to get his hands on another one.'

Fargo blew out his cheeks. 'Seems you could've picked someone more reliable when there's so much at stake.'

He felt Noble's old eyes boring into him. 'I done the best I could in the time we had. That gal ain't here very often or for long. Mostly she's away at that school of hers. Anyway, you leave Gabe Luckett to me.'

Fargo paused gnawing the last rabbit bone. 'What you gonna do?'

'Try to find him before Ohlrig does.'

'Then what?'

There was no answer and Fargo hipped on the log, frowning as he stared into blackness, but saw the empty tin plate and the spoon had been placed within his reach.

Sam Noble had simply faded away into the Brazos night.

It was past midnight when a dark rider came into the yard of the Rocking R without undue noise and quit the saddle down by the south corral where there were few horses at present. He looped the reins loosely over the fence rail, eased the cinch on the sweating, blowing animal, snatched a blanket from several that were kept draped over the top rails and covered the horse quickly.

Then he hurried around the long bunkhouse to a small extra room that had been built on the rear with its own entrance. This was Rip Ohlrig's private little world and he wasn't pleased at being disturbed by the persistent hammering on the door.

'Who the hell is that?'

'Micky Gann, Rip.' The wrangler's voice sounded breathless. 'There's somethin' you oughta know. Fact, Mr Rockwell should know but I din' wanta disturb him.'

'So you disturbed me. It better be good, Mick, or you ain't gonna be able to ride for a week.'

'It's good – or bad. Dependin' how you feel about. Lee Fargo.'

That got Rip out of bed fast and the door was wrenched open and Gann dragged inside. There was little light but the ramrod touched a vesta to a candle stub and looked at the wrangler, seeing he was dishevelled and sweaty.

'Well?'

Gann swallowed. 'I-I been keepin' an eye on Fargo like you told me, Rip. Figured I'd go over to the draw an' see what he was up to, campin' by himself – but he weren't by himself. There was a feller with him, hidin' in the dark, but from where I was I could make him out now and again when the fire flickered and showed him up. It's that silver-haired feller in the buckskins. I caught a whiff of him and—'

He had Rip's full attention now. 'What was he doin'?'

'Talkin' with Fargo. Only caught a few words but

seems Fargo wants to get into the boss's office and look for some kinda papers.'

Ohlrig was plainly puzzled. 'What papers?'

'Dunno. Couldn't get too close in case they seen or heard me. I know that buckskin *hombre* – years ago he worked on Rockin' R. Fellers always said he was hidin'- out. This was back in the days of Brent Rockwell, Kent's older brother; before your time. . . .'

'Was this silver-hair named Noble?'

'We just called him "Silver" but I heard the name, Noble, mentioned. Claimed he'd been a buff'lo runner but was wounded by Injuns and couldn't hunt no more.'

'And he's back – he's been sighted a couple of times. Boss knows him and don't like it. Don't s'pose you had the guts to follow him and see where he's holed-up?'

Mickey Gann just shook his head.

Lee Fargo was standing a'top a felled hickory, stripping the branches, when he saw the dust of a small group of riders approaching the draw.

He was bare to the waist, shirt and sixgun rig hang- ing from a nearby bush. He thunked the double-bitted axe into the fallen tree, jumped down and used a rag he kept for the purpose to wipe sweat from his chest and hard-muscled arms. By the time he had his shirt on and was buckling his gunbelt around his slim waist, he could see the riders.

Three of them. One was Rip Ohlrig, another he was pretty sure was little Mickey Gann and the third – he arched his eyebrows.

The third rider was Kent Rockwell.

He walked into his camp and waited for them there. They didn't return his brief greeting and all three looked grim, but Gann seemed kind of shifty and nervous, too.

'You ain't finished yet,' growled Rip Ohlrig, gesturing to a few trees in the area to be cleared that were still standing.

'I'll finish today – if I don't get too many interruptions.'

'Watch your mouth!' snapped Ohlrig. 'This is Mr Rockwell you're talkin' to and if he wants to interrupt you, you ain't got no say in the matter.'

Once again, there was only that maddening, stoical acceptance on Fargo's grimed face and he flicked his blue eyes to Rockwell. 'You want to see me, boss?'

'I am seein' you,' Kent said tightly, threw a glance around the small neat camp. 'But I don't see Sam Noble.'

Fargo's expression didn't change. 'Who's he?'

Rip jammed home his spurs and jumped his mount forward. It caught Fargo off-guard and the animal slammed into him, knocking him sprawling. By that time Ohlrig was out of the saddle and advancing, a brightness in his eyes at the prospect of violence. He tugged his workgloves tightly over his knuckles, but it was his boot that caught the young wrangler in the side and sent him skidding across the ground.

Mickey Gann swallowed and licked his lips: he wanted Fargo fired, but he had never taken much to Ohlrig's methods. Kent Rockwell was leaning forward in the saddle, hands folded on the horn, watching closely as the big, brutal foreman went after young Fargo.

He kicked him again and closed for a third, fists cocked, ready. But Fargo bounced to hands and knees, launched himself as if shot from a cannon, and rammed his head into Ohlrig's midriff. The foreman was surprised, staggered back, legs going wildly as he fought to keep balance. But Fargo kept shouldering into him, forcing him backwards until the man couldn't stay upright and they went down with a crash. Rip, used to rough-and-tumble, swung a backhand blow at Fargo's face that would have smashed his nose to the back of his head if it had landed. But Fargo moved with the speed of a snake and although the knuckles made his ear sing they didn't connect solidly. He hooked an elbow against the side of Ohlrig's neck and the man's head jerked and the world went all askew momentarily as blood was cut off from his brain. He felt himself fading but then consciousness came back with a rush and he forked his fingers, stabbing at Fargo's eyes.

The horny nails ripped Lee's cheek and he smashed his forehead into Rip's nose. It crunched and blood spurted and Mickey Gann cried out aloud, startled: *no one had ever seen the colour of Rip Ohlrig's blood before!*

Even Kent Rockwell frowned and dropped his jaw a little. Ohlrig himself was sure surprised and the feel of warm blood oozing over his chin brought a surge of maniacal rage. He roared and kicked and thrashed and punched and hooked and rolled until he was free of Fargo and then stumbled upright and, shirtfront red with his blood now, charged back in, arms swinging.

Some of his blows had hurt Fargo but suddenly the man jumped into the air and came at the startled Ohlrig with arms and legs flailing. The ramrod tried to change the direction of his charge but was too late. Fargo hit him and locked arms and legs about him, clamping tight, the force of his momentum carrying them both to the ground.

They rolled and Ohlrig instinctively used his knees and boots and elbows and even his teeth. But Fargo seemed to anticipate his moves and was always just out of reach or retreating so swiftly that any blow Rip did land lacked force. The ramrod was startled to find himself thrown over Fargo's hip and he crashed hard to the ground on his back. But Fargo had held on to his wrist and bent it painfully before dropping on to the man's chest with one knee.

He straddled the battered foreman, drew back his right arm, elbow crooked, knuckles white and prominent, aiming at Rip's fairly conspicuous Adam's apple – it was a vicious, savage blow, meant to kill. . . .

But Kent Rockwell heeled his mount forward, leaned from the saddle and gunwhipped Fargo brutally. The sixgun's barrel crushed his hat and the young wrangler arched his back and crashed forward. Rip Ohlrig was too dazed to push him away, but at a snapped command from Rockwell, Mickey Gann hurriedly dismounted and heaved the unconscious Fargo off Rip.

He tried to help Ohlrig up but the man smashed his proffered hand aside, snarling and spitting blood and a chipped tooth. He made several attempts before he managed to stagger upright, swaying, blood and murder roaring in his head.

He moved in on Fargo's still form, making a whining sound like a hurt animal, and began kicking the downed man methodically, grunting with each blow, pinkish spittle flying.

'Rip!' Kent snapped, repeated it several times and when Ohlrig continued to kick, he urged his mount alongside the crazed foreman and used the horse's weight to shoulder him aside. Rip sat down heavily, glared up through the blood masking his face. Panting, he staggered to his feet, still wildly angry.

'I'll ... kill ... that ... son of a ... bitch!' he croaked, but Kent kept his mount between him and Fargo.

'Mebbe later – first he's got to be made to talk.'

That seemed to get through to Ohlrig and he stopped trying to dodge around the rancher's mount. He even managed a half-grin through the blood.

'Be my ... pleasure to ... make him!'

Mickey Gann cleared his throat and said, 'Boss, you see the way that Fargo was fightin'?'

Rockwell glared and nodded curtly. 'Yeah – like a goddamn Injun! Comanche style!'

6
Pursued

The voice came to Fargo as if he was at the bottom of a deep well.

'Where's Noble's camp?' A hard hand twisted up his shirtfront and shook him until he thought his head would fly off his shoulders. He groaned and the shaking stopped and the voice roared against his ear this time: 'Where . . . is . . . Noble's camp?'

He opened his eyes and it was all fuzzy and blurred, just a couple of shadows moving indistinctly. Brutal knuckles slammed across his face, twisting his head on his neck, and he spat a little blood and then the hand came swinging back and smacked his head around the other way.

He looked straight into the inflexible face of Kent Rockwell with its iron-bound expression. 'Better talk, boy. You'll get tired of this a lot quicker than Rip.'

'Already . . . tired of it,' gasped Fargo. 'But I . . . dunno where Sam is.'

He braced himself for a blow and saw Ohlrig draw back his right fist, but a finger raised by the rancher made him pause. 'At least he's no longer pretending he doesn't know who Noble is – and maybe he doesn't know where he's holed-up.' He nudged Fargo roughly. 'Just what is Noble to you, kid?'

Fargo turned his head slowly – his neck was stiff and sore – and he glimpsed Mickey Gann standing behind the rancher. The old wrangler looked kind of uncomfortable but he said nothing. Lee started to speak, stopped, then, apparently making up his mind, looked directly into Rockwell's face and said, 'Guess I owe him my life. He snatched me away from some Comanches just before an army troop rode in and wiped 'em out.'

Rockwell stiffened and paled. Rip Ohlrig frowned but Gann pursed his lips thoughtfully.

'The hell were you doin' with Comanches?' Ohlrig snapped.

'Living with 'em. Seems they took me when I was just a shaver – reared me in their ways, but I was never fully accepted by 'em.'

'They call you – Tall Wolf?' grated Rockwell, referring to the painted symbol on the headband.

Surprised, Lee nodded. 'Tall *Dog* it was first – most Comanche are squat build – I was taller than any of 'em and they didn't care for it, slapped the tag on me as a kind of insult. I was never kind of taken in to a group. I was always just a little bit *out* of it. It was only after I had a vision that they changed my name to Tall Wolf. . . .'

'Why din' they just kill you?'

Fargo swivelled his gaze to Rip Ohlrig. 'Because they

needed men – they're always short of men to fight for
them. That's why they don't mind taking a white child,
boy or girl, and rearing them in their ways. Sooner or
later the boy will grow into a man and the girl will give
them babies when she becomes a woman.'

'I'd cut the throat of any woman I thought'd been
with a stinkin' Comanche!' Rip Ohlrig said bitterly.

'Your name,' cut in Rockwell suddenly. 'What was,
your white name?'

Fargo hesitated. 'I dunno. Too young to remember, I
guess . . . I had a few flashes of memory – a man with a
big moustache sitting me on a paint pony. A woman
with hair black as midnight. She smiled a lot. . . .'

'What else d'you recall?' Rockwell snapped, his voice
hoarse. Then suddenly he wheeled and glared at
Mickey Gann, as if just remembering his presence. 'You
go back to the mustang camp or the ranch. You ain't
needed here any longer.'

Gann opened his mouth to speak, caught the
narrowed look that Rip threw him, swallowed and
nodded, walking back to his horse. They all watched
him ride away.

'Well. . . ?'

Fargo shook his aching head. 'I dunno – things came
to me in dreams. I can't remember. They didn't matter
to me.'

'How old are you?'

'Sam says I'm about twenty-three or twenty-four. I'd
have to believe him; I don't have any idea.'

Rockwell studied him hard and long. 'I think you're
lyin'.'

'I'll beat the truth outa him, boss!' Ohlrig cocked his fist again but Rockwell took something from his pocket, thrust his fist towards Fargo, then uncurled his fingers. The silver dollar with the R balanced on a short arc glittered in the sun. Fargo stared at it and lifted his gaze to the rancher's face.

'Where'd you get that?' he asked softly.

'From your warbag. What I want to know is where *you* got it.'

'Had it all my life. Was tied round my neck by a leather thong when the Comanche took me in, or so they told me.' Fargo hesitated and then added, 'Sam Noble recognized it, too. He was about to beat my brains out when he saw it and recognized it. It saved my life, I guess.'

Rockwell swore. 'Damn Noble! You know what it means?'

'It's my totem,' Fargo said, face serious beneath the bruises and cuts. 'It protects me from bad medicine.'

Ohlrig spat and hit him in the face, flinging him away so that he sprawled on the ground. 'Quit that Injun hogwash! You answer Mr Rockwell proper, or—'

Ohlrig made a menacing move towards his gun with his hand and then Fargo kicked out, one boot catching Rip on the left knee-cap. The ramrod yelled in pain and the leg collapsed and Fargo jumped up and lifted a knee into Ohlrig's face. The man floundered back, arms flung wide, and Fargo whirled at the sound of gun metal sliding against leather.

Rockwell had drawn his pistol and even as Fargo dropped to one knee the rancher fired and the bullet whispered past Fargo's face. The rancher lifted the gun for a second shot and then there was a blazing sixgun in Fargo's hand.

Rockwell staggered away, clawing at his right upper arm, his gun falling from numbed fingers. He swung back, face contorted, eyes wide, clearly waiting for Fargo to take the killing shot. But Fargo merely covered him with the cocked gun, stooped without taking his eyes off the rancher and picked up the silver dollar. He slipped it into his pocket.

'Feel better now. Sam Noble said it was my father hung that coin round my neck. Had something to do with my legacy. . . .' Fargo smiled crookedly at the big rancher whose sleeve was soaked with blood now. 'The sign on it looks just like the Rocking R brand, Rockwell—'

'Get out.' Rockwell gritted. 'Get off my land! You're fired! You ever show your nose around these parts again you'll be shot on sight. Them's the orders I aim to give to every man who rides for me, so you'd do well to stay right away from here, mister – whoever you are!'

'Sounds kind of final. Well, maybe I'll stay away, then again maybe I won't. . . . You know, for a while, after Sam took me away from the Comanche, I wasn't interested in finding out about my whiteman life. I went back to live with a different tribe for a while: even went on my first war-party. Sam had confused me: for years I knew I was white, but I had no name, no one I knew who was white and might care about me. I drifted a spell, then one night Sam walked into my camp again – and this time I stayed with him. And he brought me here. You know Sam right well, don't you, Rockwell?'

'I should've killed the son of a bitch years ago! I heard he was dead and was stupid enough to believe it. I ought to've gone lookin' for his body!'

'Or maybe you mean – mine?'

Rockwell's eyes flashed. 'I dunno what the hell you're talkin' about.' He shook a bloodstained finger at the young wrangler. 'You been told! Git off Rockin' R!'

Fargo smiled thinly, walked forward and gun-whipped Rockwell, leaving the man on hands and knees, holding his throbbing head, moaning. 'I'll be back – and you know why!'

Then he turned and was in time to see Rip Ohlrig making a dive for his dropped gun. He kicked the ramrod in the ribs, then slammed his gun barrel across his head.

When Fargo rode out, he took Rockwell and Ohlrig's horses with him, turning them loose in heavy timber.

Sam'l Houston Noble was ashamed of himself.

He had lived in the wilderness most of his life and he had prided himself that when he made a camp he didn't want anyone to find, then by hell not even the Devil himself could track him down.

Yet here he was, jumped and cornered by two of the dumbest sons of bitches that ever came down the river.

The Luckett brothers. Filthy, reeking of booze and looking wild-eyed because they didn't have any more – and with guns in their hands. Gabe had an old sixgun but Rance had a shotgun and if there was anyone meaner than Gabe it was Rance.

They'd caught him flat-footed. He'd been lying atop a big boulder, using his old brass-and-leather telescope to watch Fargo's camp far below in the draw. He saw Rockwell and Ohlrig and Mickey Gann arrive and later, Mickey leave.

Noble had smiled to himself when Fargo had all but beaten Rip Ohlrig – he'd bet that damn ramrod had wondered what had hit him when Fargo had used those Indian fighting ways.

Deciding he would get closer in case Fargo needed a hand – and he sure looked as if he did the way Rockwell had gunwhipped him and Ohlrig had started in to kick him – he was sliding down backwards from the boulder when he heard the gun hammers cocking. He whirled, groping for his rifle, battered and scratched after years of use and with the receiver covered by decorated rawhide, held in place by glue obtained from boiling-down deer hoofs.

'Don't be stupid, Noble!' growled Rance Luckett, and then Gabe had come at him from the side, gunwhipped him to his knees and taken his sixgun.

Now they pushed and shoved him back up the slope to where his camp was and Gabe kicked his legs out from under him and told him to stay put on the ground beside the coals of the smokeless camp-fire.

'Out of luck if you're lookin' for dinero,' Noble said, and Gabe kicked him in the ribs.

'Shut up till we tell you to talk!'

Rance hooked a hip over one end of a low boulder, but the shotgun covered Noble all the time. 'Lookin' for Lee Fargo – leastways, we know where he is in that draw, but we figured before we go see him you might tell us just what in hell you two are up to.'

Noble said nothing and that earned him another kick from Gabe and he was told to answer or get stomped-on.

'Lee got himself a job on Rockin' R – I just been hangin' around, kinda keepin' an eye on things. That Rip Ohlrig's a mean snake.' Noble lifted his eyes to Gabe. 'You knew Lee was anglin' for a job when we paid you to frighten that gal.'

Gabe, hung-over and needing a drink badly, grunted and started going through the mountain man's gear, but Noble never carried booze. Rance watched for a couple of minutes then jerked the shotgun barrels.

'You go sit with your back to that tree.' And when Noble was in position he said, 'There's somethin' queer about the way you set things up for Fargo to get that job, playin' the hero and so on; we wanna know what it is.'

Noble shrugged. 'Kid had tried for other jobs but they're hard to come by. Just figured this way he would likely get a job if he asked.'

'You're lyin'!' Rance snapped and Gabe turned from searching the old man's buckskin 'possibles' bag, flung it away and started across the slope, eager to have someone on whom to take out his frustration. 'You an' the kid're up to somethin', gonna make a lot of money outa Rockwell – I smell it. We want to be cut in.' Rance smiled crookedly. 'Or maybe we might just mosey on down and tell Rockwell about you siccin' Gabe on to his daughter – that'd spoil things for you!'

'I dunno what the hell you're talkin' about.'

Gabe snarled and, within a few steps of Noble, ran at the man, clawed hands reaching for his wrinkled neck. But the Lucketts had made a big mistake. They had taken Noble's sixgun, but had left him his big Bowie hunting knife.

And now he reached around behind him in a quick movement and Gabe stopped dead, lifting to his toes, a rising scream choked off by bubbling blood as he ran on to the big blade. His sixgun triggered as Noble grabbed at him.

Rance blinked and jumped to his feet, lurching to one side and firing one barrel of the shotgun. Noble swung the sagging Gabe around and the man's body was wrenched from him by the charge of buckshot and flung brokenly across the camp. Rance stared in horror at what he had done and Noble lunged for the rifle, sliding and rolling downslope, snatching it up, twisting on to his back, working lever and trigger. Rance staggered back and jerked and his shotgun blasted as he fell to one knee, sagging slowly, blood oozing through his ragged shirt front.

Sam'l Houston Noble was kicked several feet down the slope by the buckshot and it twisted him on to his side so that he lay there with knees drawn up, life blood seeping into the earth through his torn buckskins. . . .

Lee Fargo reined-down abruptly, fighting the protesting horse as the bit sawed at its mouth. He heard the gunfire from up on the mountain, sixgun, rifle and shotgun – something told him it came from Noble's camp and he spurred the horse on just as it settled down from the sudden stop.

It protested again with a whinny and then at another touch of the spurs, bunched muscles and started up through the timber. . . .

Mickey Gann heard the gunfire, too. He had been heading back slowly towards the ranch house, feeling offended by the way Rockwell had dismissed him just as he had started to question Fargo, when he heard the shooting from the draw.

He knew they had either killed Fargo or – what? Other way about? Fargo had killed Rockwell and Rip? Wounded them . . . ?

Then he heard the horses and saw Fargo leading the other two mounts out of the draw and starting up the slope. Gann hesitated – the draw? Or follow Fargo?

He decided to follow Fargo even before the young wrangler turned loose Rockwell and Ohlrig's horses. They would graze a spell, might even find their way back to the draw. And Fargo wouldn't have taken them if Rockwell and Rip were dead. The hell with them, anyway! They were treating him like dirt – Rockwell especially, for the man must have seen the way Gann had looked at that silver dollar, recalled that he had been just an ordinary run-of-the-mill bronc-buster way back when big brother Brent ran things. *That* was why he had ordered him out of the draw: didn't want him remembering.

Just in case he remembered *too much* about that time. It only confirmed what Mickey Gann had been thinking about; this mystery man who called himself Lee Fargo. . . .

It was about then that he heard the shooting from up on the mountain, saw Fargo put his horse up the steep slope, spurring and lashing with the rein ends.

That decided Gann: he spun his mount and set out to follow Fargo, letting him get a good way ahead, but still keeping him in sight.

Noble was still alive, but Fargo, kneeling beside the old man, knew he wouldn't last long.

The buckshot had torn him up too much and Fargo simply couldn't stop the bleeding. Too many veins and arteries and organs had been damaged, but he did what he was able to, holding a wadded spare shirt from his saddle-bag against the deep wound. Noble groaned and his eyes fluttered half open, glazed-over.

'Can . . . hardly see. That you . . . Lee?'

'It's me, Sam. You got both the Lucketts.'

Noble gave a small grunt and his head moved, but whether it was a nod or just his neck muscles growing weaker, the young wrangler wasn't sure. 'Sam, it's a bad wound.'

This time it was a definite nod. 'Know that. Been holdin' . . . on . . . hopin' you'd come, but don't waste too much time on me. . . The . . . the Bowie. . . .'

One hand flapped a few inches and Fargo glanced across to where the torn body of Gabe Luckett lay, the big knife still protruding from his chest. 'It's still in Gabe, Sam.'

'H-handle . . . hollow. Map – gold. Stashed it – bit by

. . . bit over . . . years. Allus . . . figured . . . give grand-kids one . . . day. San Antone. K-Kyle and Jo P-Preston. . . .'

'I'll get it to 'em, Sam.'

One withered, bloodstained hand tugged feebly at his shirt sleeve. 'You . . . use . . . some. Go . . . Waco—'

'I'm not running away, Sam. Not after all you've done for me. And what they did to you.'

The old head rolled from side to side. 'Rosa Reynola – She. . . .'

The voice trailed off and Fargo leaned closer. 'Sam? Who's Rosa Reynola?'

'M-mother – *your* moth. . . .'

He slumped and Fargo knew he would learn no more.

7
Man of Mystery

The only tool he had for digging a grave was the Bowie knife. He pulled it from Gabe Luckett's chest, and found that the leatherbound handle did indeed turn on a threaded though slim tang. He didn't unscrew it all the way, just satisfied himself that Noble hadn't been raving, that there was a rolled paper in the hollow tube.

He heaved aside a fallen tree, propped it up with rocks and dug out a shallow grave from the depression left by the log. He dragged Noble's body across and arranged him on his back, hands folded across his chest. There was no white-man's prayer that he cared to say, but he knelt on one knee and lifted his arms wide to the sky, singing softly to the Great Spirit, asking that Old Sam Noble be taken into His care, to give him green plains to roam and many fine animals to hunt and the comfort of a true woman when needed. From a pocket he took a beaded necklace strung on rawhide and placed it under the old man's hands.

Then he filled in the grave and rolled the tree back in place. Under the circumstances it was as near as he could come to the Comanche custom of driving a warrior's herd of horses over and over the grave until it was obliterated and became one with the earth around it.

When he straightened and wiped dirt from the now ruined Bowie blade and sheathed it, he saw movement at the edge of the trees. His hand flashed to his gun butt and the weapon covered the startled man watching from the edge of the clearing.

It was Mickey Gann.

The wrangler blew out his cheeks as he raised his hands halfway to his shoulders. 'Man, you never learned to draw like that livin' with no Comanche!'

Fargo narrowed his eyes, as if making up his mind whether to shoot Gann or not. He lowered the hammer and sheathed the gun. 'Sam taught me.'

Gann nodded soberly. 'Yeah – he used to be lightnin' fast in the old days before he took to the mountains.'

'You knew him back then?'

'Yeah – I was bronc-buster and saddler on the Rockin' R at that time. Run by the two Rockwell brothers, Brent, the elder, and Kent. . . .' Suddenly he looked sly and gave a crooked smile. 'You're Gideon, ain't you?'

Fargo's expression didn't change. 'Gideon who?'

Gann laughed shortly. 'OK – leave it ride. Now the Lucketts've finally nailed Noble, and you been fired by Kent. What you gonna do next?'

'I have somewhere to go.'

'Sam told you somethin' before he went to glory, huh?'

'Just get on your way, Mickey. I've got nothing to say to you.'

'Mebbe not – mebbe there's somethin' I can say to you.' Gann waited but Fargo merely stared deadpan at him and the old wrangler said, 'Dunno how much you know about Noble, but, like I said, he was handy with a gun in his young days – and he killed a few men. One was said to be cold-blooded murder although he always claimed he was set-up for it and there was one man who could give him an alibi.'

Fargo was interested now.

'Wounded and on the run, he come to Rockin' R. Brent was away buyin' cows and for some reason Kent took him in – aimed to use him, I guess. He was always the sharpest of the brothers and didn't mind bendin' the law. He used what he knew about Sam to pressure him into doin' some illegal chores for him. Sam had no choice. He din' like it but din' dare run. Him and Brent got along OK but Kent was the one used him.'

'Believe he told me as much but didn't go into detail.'

'Well, only one chore really mattered: Kent and Brent were always arguin', specially over the way Kent brought in cows with other men's brands on 'em and even ran quite a few small ranchers off their land. Brent did a lot of travellin', buyin' good stock, and while he was away Kent did what he liked. Well, come to a real ding-dong, knock-down, drag-out fight and Kent got beat to a pulp, but they seemed to make it up afterwards, like they'd reached some sort of an under-standin'. You know all this?'

'Keep talking.' Fargo looked around the slope as if he might be expecting some sort of pursuit, but turned back when Gann started to speak again.

'Word got out that the fight had been because Brent told Kent he'd married while away on one of his trips, married a Mexican woman and he even had a son – just a few months old. Everythin' seemed to be goin' along fine and they started buildin' a new part on the ranch for Brent's wife and the baby. Like I said, I was saddler as well as, bronc-buster, and Kent – he never give me the time of day usually, was the same with most of the crew except his own special bunch of hardcases – anyways, he come to where I was workin' on a bridle one day and asked me if I had many saddles needin' attention. Thought he must have some other chore for me and I told him there was three for repair but, only one was real bad, stitchin' all busted on a cinchstrap, leather near worn through at the ring. The other two could be used in safety but not that one. He said OK and walked away.'

Fargo was a little more intense in his attitude now. He said quietly, 'Sam told me Brent was killed while riding – cinchstrap broke and he and his horse went off a high trail.'

Gann smiled crookedly. 'You ain't dumb, are you? Yeah, Kent insisted on saddlin' Brent's hoss that day and after Brent had gone to bring back his wife and kid, I noticed the saddle with the busted cinch was missin'. I told Kent but he said to forget it, and finish my chores.

It'd turn up.' He paused. 'And it did. In the gulch, on the hoss Brent'd been ridin', busted to glory. Killed both man and hoss, that fall.'

'If you're inferring Kent arranged Brent's death, how could he have known the cinchstrap would break in a dangerous place like that high trail?'

Gann looked cunning. 'Mebbe he didn't – mebbe he seen to it that Brent went off the trail first, *then* the hoss went – the fall would bust the strap and who'd know when it happened, before or after the fall. . . ?'

'That's accusing a man of murder, Mickey.' Fargo's voice was flat.

'You knew that story before, didn't you? Sam told you. He must've, if you were with him long as you say.'

'It's about seven years since he rescued me from the Comanche – not that I *wanted* to be rescued. I'd grown-up with the Indians, didn't know any other life, but Sam taught me how to live as a whiteman. Can't say I liked it much. I took off now and again, tried to find a tribe I could live with, but the ones who'd reared me had been mostly wiped-out by the soldiers. In the end, I went back and stayed with Sam.'

'And he set it up for Gabe to attack Liza Rockwell so's you could "rescue" her and get yourself a job on Rockin' R. Now I wonder why he done that?'

Fargo said nothing, figuring just what to do about Gann now.

'Like I said, I reckon you're Gideon.'

'I don't know any Gideon. My name's Lee Fargo and I've a long ways to go, so you'd best be on your way, Mickey. Your job's safe now that I'm going.'

'You gonna be comin' back?' Gann asked tautly.

'Who knows?'

Gann looked thoughtful and Fargo knew the man was weighing up the pros and cons before he decided upon his next course of action.

'You didn't say what special chore Sam had to do for Kent,' Fargo said, and there was an edge to his voice and Gann's smile widened.

'Gotcha, ain't I? You know what's comin'. Sam must've told you.'

Fargo was silent a moment, then said, 'Maybe I just want to check it out.'

Gann snorted. 'Well, no one on Rockin' R knew for sure what happened, but I kinda figured it out. Brent was goin' to collect his wife and son, right? Well, it was a cinch the kid was gonna inherit Brent's share if and when Brent died – and everyone knew Kent had big plans for Rockin' R and was lookin' forward to ownin' the whole kit and caboodle some fine day. . . . Brent cramped his style, you see?'

'So he wouldn't want Brent's son in the picture.'

'Right. Sam was obliged to him and more or less under Kent's thumb because he was still hidin' him out from that murder he thought they still wanted him for. His job was to go meet Brent's wife and kid – and make sure neither of 'em reached Rockin' R.'

His eyes flashed but he needn't have worried – he had Fargo's full attention.

'Sam came back and said he'd taken care of it.'

'Did he say how?' Fargo's voice sounded kind of strangled and his nostrils were pinched as he leaned forward a little, eager for Gann's answer.

'Didn't Sam tell you that?'

'*You* tell me!'

'Well, I dunno for sure, but I guess Sam said he left the woman and baby way out in the desert without food or water. Or that he killed 'em and buried 'em where the bodies'd never be found. Whatever it was, it satisfied Kent. And he believed Brent's wife and son were dead all these years – then you turn up, carryin' a silver dollar for that year – 1861 – that Brent'd marked with the Rockin' R brand and that the kid was s'posed to be wearin' round his neck on a leather thong. Symbol of his legacy, I guess. Kid's name was Gideon, but I *know* Sam must've told you that.' He laughed. 'How'd I do? My story check out with Noble's all right?'

'And Kent thinks I'm his nephew come back to claim my legacy, is that it?'

'Well – ain't you?'

'Don't seem to matter much whether I am or not. If Kent *believes* I am, he's gonna want me dead.'

'Mebbe I can help.' Fargo waited for more. 'Like I can tell you if you was hopin' to get a look at Brent's Will namin' you as his heir, you can save your time – Kent made sure every copy of that Will was destroyed right after Brent's death. Maybe we can do some kinda deal, eh?'

Impatiently, Fargo pushed past the wrangler and made for his horse standing just inside the line of trees. He heard Gann's gun coming out of leather, whirled, but didn't draw his own sixgun. He jumped the short distance between them, using his superior body weight to knock Mickey off his feet. Fargo reached down and twisted the gun out of Gann's small, calloused hand. The man looked up at him, fear in his eyes now.

'Decide it was better to kill me and stay in Kent's good books than to let me go and take the chance I might be back, Mickey?'

Gann said nothing, swallowed. He winced and put his hands up in front of his face as Fargo hefted the gun. Then the young cowboy swore briefly and slugged Mickey across the side of the head. The man slammed over sideways, twitching a little. Fargo hesitated, then hit him again behind the ear and the wrangler lay still, breathing raggedly.

Lee Fargo was gone from the camp in minutes, pausing only briefly to raise a farewell hand towards Sam Noble's last resting place.

The map was old and barely legible, but Fargo had been on Rocking R long enough to recognize landmarks. He lined them up but missed one at first and had to double back. He reined in on a flat ledge and studied the map again, saw where he had gone wrong, worked out in his head the trail he would need to take down to the draw where Sam had marked the hiding place of the gold.

The old mountain man had mentioned a couple of times that he had had a little luck prospecting and had stashed the gold, aiming to send it to his grandchildren, Kyle and Jo Preston, in San Antonio, when he had enough to make it worthwhile.

He had never mentioned their mother except to say

she had died right after the girl had been born and the father, destroyed by grief, had run off and never been heard of again. They had been brought up in orphanages and he had always felt guilty that he had done nothing to help them have a decent life. But he had somehow kept track of them. . . .

'You ain't very curious are you, kid?' he said once after talking about the gold. When Fargo – called "Wolf" or "kid" by Noble at that time – asked what he meant, Noble had added, 'You ain't asked where I stashed it.'

'None of my business.'

'Might be one day,' Noble said enigmatically. 'But I figured I might's well let Kent look after it for me till I want it.'

Fargo had wondered what he meant and now he knew: the gold was hidden on Rocking R land. It had meant something to Noble, stashing it out on Kent Rockwell's ranch. . . .

Now Fargo started to put the map in his shirt pocket before moving down off the ledge and, as he lifted his hand there was a rifle shot and the bullet buzzed past his face so close that he jerked his head back and, involuntarily lifted the reins at the same time.

His mount took it as a signal and plunged down the steep slope with a wild whinny.

Rocking in the saddle, Fargo strained, legs straight out in the stirrups, leaning his upper body backwards so that the mount wouldn't have too much weight forward and run a greater risk of tumbling. The rear legs were folded now and dust and gravel shot up and to the side. If the rifleman was still shooting at him he could neither hear the shots nor see where the bullets went – he was in the midst of too much turmoil, plunging down the near-vertical slope, expecting to crash any second. Branches whipped and slashed at his face.

There were deadfalls sprawled across this part of the slope and he wrenched on the reins, used his knees and spurs to manoeuvre around them. Once he tried to lift the horse over a long log and they almost went down but somehow the animal regained its feet and did little more than *step* across.

Then the hell-for-leather descent started again.

He managed to glance over his shoulder once and he saw three riders up on the ledge he had departed so abruptly.

I should've put a bullet in you, Mickey! he thought.

Gann had led Rockwell and Ohlrig into the mountains on his trail.

Then there was brush tearing at his legs and the horse was wrenching its head this way and that to keep from being stabbed in the eyes and mouth by the branches. He heard the *thruuupppp!* of a bullet passing his head and knew they were still trying to stop his escape. Once on the flat and in the midst of the brush, he hauled rein long enough to stand in the stirrups and look back.

They were running their mounts across the ledge, looking for the regular trail down.

He found he was still clutching the crumpled map in his hand and, not wanting them to find this on him if they ran him down, reached up and pushed it deep into the rotted bole of a live oak. Ants were on his hand when he withdrew it and he shook them off. The map would be destroyed eventually but he knew now where to look for the gold. It would still be there when – or if – he came back.

And he knew he had to get out of this country that Rockwell and the others knew so much better than he did or he would be cornered and killed. Rockwell had nothing to lose by his death, but everything to gain.

He heard them coming, nearly at the bottom already, wrenched his shaking, panting mount's head around and plunged away towards the south-west. If he could make it as far as the edge of the desert he would be on the fringe of country he had roamed as a Comanche.

It would be almost like going home.

8

Second Time Unlucky

He wasn't sure that they were trying to kill him so much as trying to stop him.

Every now and again there was shooting and the bullets ranged pretty close, but most seemed on a level that were meant for his horse. Only the odd one or two whined overhead. He looked back several times and it seemed to be Rip Ohlrig doing most of the shooting, although Mickey Gann had dismounted a couple of times to try his luck. Kent Rockwell had a rifle, too, but whatever shooting he did was from the saddle. Casual. Indifferent.

Fargo figured he could outrun them – if his horse was in better shape. But that wild plunge down the steep slope had taken a deal out of the animal, scraped off a lot of hide, and spooked the horse. Now it tended to balk whenever a sharp bend came up and he had to saw with the reins, throw his weight in the direction he wanted to go, literally pulling the horse around.

He didn't blame the animal – that wild ride down the mountain had scared him, too. Comanche were great horsemen, probably the finest of the Plains Indians, and they cared for their mounts, painted them with symbols, saw they were fed well: he knew, because it had been his job along with Rain Lover and Like A Pine Tree and the other youths to watch over the herds of horses. If any warrior figured his mount hadn't had proper attention the youth responsible suffered plenty – not just pain but humiliation. His mouth tightened at remembered penance, always made worse because, unlike the other males in the tribe, he was starting to show signs of the mark of the whiteman that the Comanche despised the most – the hair-growth on the face. None of the Indians grew facial hair. If the occasional one showed even a smudge of fluff it was swiftly removed – not just with a sharp blade, but by running a twist of grass-string all over the affected area until the lay of the string had pulled every last vestige of hair out by the roots . . . and not without pain.

Fargo brought himself back to the present with a jerk: for a few moments there he had again been living those distant days with the tribe. Now they were long gone and only a few Comanche roamed free and rebellious – like most of the Indian tribes, the survivors of the deliberately contrived slaughters of five years ago had been herded on to reservations, worthless land the whitemen had no use for.

Now, as two bullets passed over his head, he felt a sadness – for even if he made it to the old Comanche country, he doubted he would find any free-ranging groups who could – or would – help him.

But he had no intention of letting Kent Rockwell get his hands on him.

It had seemed like a good idea at first, claiming back his legacy that Kent Rockwell had stolen from him. He had never doubted Sam Noble's story for even when the moutain man had taken him prisoner he had felt respect for the oldster. He had seen him before, running his traplines in the hills, staying away from the Indians, taking only what animals he needed, living close to the Earth Spirit like the Comanche. A few youths had sought his scalp once or twice, but he had fought well and most of the rash young men had learned a harsh lesson, some getting their wish and dying in battle before going to the Happy Hunting Grounds. . . .

Sam's story had been hard to follow at first. It was only later, when he learned the whiteman's language – his true native tongue according to Noble – did he realize what the old man had told him.

Noble skimmed over why he had been wounded and running from the law when Kent Rockwell had taken him in at Rocking R.

'Just say I was in trouble and there were dodgers out for me,' Noble had told him. 'Kent and his brother Brent ran the Rockin' R but Brent was away so much that Kent really ran things – and he got the notion that because of this the ranch really belonged to him. He didn't want to share it with Brent who was an honest man and wanted to build up a big spread with good bloodline cattle. They fought all the time over Kent's wideloopin' and land-grabbin' while brother Brent was away. . . .

'Anyway it all blew up in one big fight when Brent told Kent he'd got hisself married on one of his trips and had a son. It was never clear whether he married this Mexican woman, Rosa, before or after the kid was born but it didn't matter because all Kent saw was that Brent had an heir and half the ranch would go to the kid when Brent died – I b'lieve Kent was plannin' to kill Brent even at that stage. But Brent was a strong man, had a powerful will, and he built a special cabin on the ranch for him and his wife and son. He set out to go fetch them – and was killed along the way. It looked like an accident but I know better. Kent fixed it, murdered his own brother.'

Sam Noble had been silent for a time after that and when he continued he had spoken quietly, reluctantly.

'Kent knew I'd killed several men in the past in gunfights. He told me if I wanted to repay him for hiding me out from the law, I had to do a chore for him. It was one I didn't want. I was to go to the rendezvous where Brent was; supposed to meet his wife and son – and kill them both.' Again a long silence before continuing the story. 'I was to take them out into the desert and abandon them without food or water or horses; way, way out where, if their remains were ever found they wouldn't be able to be identified . . . I couldn't do it. The woman – well, maybe if she'd been alone I might've, but not with that little boy. I told her to go back to Mexico. She was afraid, knew Kent might hunt her down if there was even a hint she was still alive, but it was the boy she was afraid for most. She knew Kent would never stop trying to kill him. So, she asked me to find a safe place for the kid. She was willing to take her chances as long as she knew the kid was safe. Hell, I din' want that responsibility. Sam'l Houston Noble with a squallin' kid - din' bear thinkin' about. But she was a fine woman, that Rosa, and I agreed. I seen her safe to the border then I had to figure out what to do with the kid. In Biggesville, a lower Rio town that had been raided by the Comanche not long before, I heard about the Injuns stealin' white children – and I knew myself how they had often done this, raised the kids in their ways, used the boys as warriors, the girls to bear babies, help keep the tribe goin'. I was on pretty good terms with a chief named Yellow Horse and I knew his wife had just lost a baby, so I went to Yellow Horse and after a while he agreed to take the kid in, his wife eager to have a baby of her own because the birth of the other one had torn her insides up and she figured she would-n't be able to bear any more kids.

'Yellow Horse wasn't quite so keen but he wanted the woman to be happy. The kid had a talisman round its neck, a silver dollar that Brent had apparently carved with the Rockin' R brand. Yellow Horse said the kid should wear this always, a whiteman's coin, because he could never be a true Comanche. . . .'

By then Fargo knew *he* had been that child, young Gideon Rockwell, Brent's son.

'It's time you claimed your legacy, kid,' Noble had told him. 'It won't be easy and Kent will kill you first chance he gets if he knows who you are. What you have to do is see if your father's Will is still around. It ain't likely, but Kent's a hoarder and I reckon he still has the Wanted dodgers that were out on me when I first arrived at Rockin' R. If the Will is there, we can prove who you are and you'll get your share.'

'And if this . . . Will, is not there?'

Noble had smiled faintly through his silver beard. 'Then we'll have to do it another way – but we will do it, kid. We will get your legacy.'

'And I will avenge my father's murder!'

'Yellow Horse trained you well, huh? A Comanche never forgets a debt or a grudge they say—'

'Why didn't the whiteman's law punish Kent for killing my father?'

'No real proof, kid. But I know he murdered Brent and a few others on Rockin' R know it, too. I quit soon as I could get away and all this time Kent has believed you and your mother are dead. So did I until I saw that medallion swingin' round your neck six or seven years age.'

'Where is my mother?'

'That I dunno right now – I've heard of her a few times over the years. She's made her own life, or mebbe she's dead. I dunno for sure. You have to forget her – concentrate on gettin' your legacy.'

'And you will want your share, of course.'

Noble's wrinkled face had straightened. 'That ain't kind, kid! I savvy why you'd say that, but I just want to see you right, because you'll bring Kent Rockwell to his knees. That's what *I* want to see. An', well, I ain't never

been happy about leavin' you with them
Comanche. . . .'

'You have your own debt to pay, I think, Sam.'

Noble had nodded, but made no explanation. Not
then.

Fargo hadn't found out what it was for a long time.
Not until Sam had told him how Rockwell had kept him
hidden out and let him believe he was still a hunted
man and that the only man who could have cleared his
name was dead – but the man *had* actually cleared
Sam's name in a death-bed confession. Yet Kent let Sam
believe that he still had a hold over him and could force
him to do whatever he wanted.

Now there was no doubt that Kent had recognized
that silver dollar Rip Ohlrig had found in Fargo's
warbag and now knew who Fargo really was.

The stream took him by surprise. He must have swung
more to the north than he had intended. It was narrow
but deep and swirling with current. He slowed and
hipped awkwardly in the saddle. The pursuing trio had
spread out. Ohlrig was riding a ridge almost parallel to
the stream's course. Gann and Rockwell were coming
in fast along the line of brush that had first hidden the
stream from Fargo.

He could plunge the ailing mount into the water
before they were within rifle shot, but he would not
make it across before they were able to shoot at him.
There was no time to think about it: he either crossed
the stream, or stayed on this side and ran on into
narrowing canyons he did not know. He figured the

Rocking R men would know them well.

Then he suddenly wrenched the reins with a half-shouted Comanche cry, torn from him involuntarily, plunging the horse into the water. It was deep right up to the bank and the surge of current snatched at them, startling Fargo. He hadn't expected it to be this strong so close to the bank.

The water washed over his legs and into his lap. The horse snorted and pawed frantically at the moving green. Its strength had been sapped by the long chase and he could feel it tremble as it fought the current. But it was no use and the animal's instincts urged it to go with the flow. This it did, and they were carried fast downstream – still fighting only a few yards from the bank – and with Rockwell and Gann closing fast.

But he should have watched for Ohlrig.

Rip, riding along the ridge, was now almost directly above the point where Fargo entered the stream. The first Fargo realized the man was so close was when the horse jerked and whiskered and plunged, rolling. He felt the warm blood splash on him from the bullet hole torn in the arched neck and then he was going under, left boot caught in the stirrup. The horse was jerking and thrashing, likely going into a pre-death convulsion, and the green water was clouding brownish-red with the blood pulsing from the massive wound: the bullet must have hit an artery.

The horse was as good as dead and so was he if he didn't free his boot. It had twisted as he had turned to see where Gann and Rockwell were and must have slipped sideways in the oxbow as the horse rolled. He kicked and pushed at the animal's quivering body, but it was being tossed by the current and he was dragged around underneath. His lungs were raw and hot with the small amount of air still trapped in them, bursting to escape. His fingers were fumbling, straining to reach the boot.

Then something jabbed up under his ribs. At first he thought it was a snag, the slimy broken branch of a waterlogged tree, but then he realized it was the handle of Sam Noble's big Bowie knife, still rammed into his belt. He almost dropped it getting it free of the buckskin sheath but then he had it in his hand and he groped for the stirrup leather, almost blind now in the churned-up, clouded water.

His numbed fingers found the taut leather straps and bubbles burst from his lips as he arched his body, held them in his left hand, sawed with the blade. It was dulled from digging the grave for Noble and his head swam dizzily now as the blunted metal worked across the stirrup leather. He felt his grip loosening on the knife – and felt consciousness slowly slipping away. If he dropped the heavy Bowie he was a goner; if the horse sank on top of him and trapped him against the stream bed, he was a goner. . . .

And if he didn't saw through that goddamn strap in a hurry he was a goner, too!

No use. The blade was too blunt, the leather too thick and strong. But even as his pummelled body wanted to give up he was still hacking weakly with the knife.

And suddenly the leather parted at the same instant

the very last of the air exploded from his strained lungs.

He sank without its buoyancy and his boots touched the rocks on the streambed and he kicked out instinctively. . . .

He didn't remember surfacing or anything at all after that until he opened his eyes, coughing up river water, and managed to focus on the three men standing over him on the river-bank.

'Second time unlucky, kid,' Kent Rockwell told him with a tight grin. 'This was where your old man was s'posed to meet his Mexican whore – and you.' He leaned closer. 'But I can guarantee you won't ever see this place a third time!'

9
The Desert

Lee Fargo's arms felt as if they were being pulled out of their sockets. But he knew if he let go his failing grip on the rope he would begin to roll and the hide would be flayed off him by the sand and grit.

And Rip Ohlrig was making no effort to dodge the hard-packed humps of earth that had spikey, dried sticks protruding, or razor-edged grass, sun-baked and wounding.

He coughed almost incessantly, choked by the gritty dust and small clods kicked up by Rip's galloping horse as it was spurred deeper into the desert. The rope was cutting into his wrists and forearms and also around his chest. His arm muscles were cracking with strain, aching with the first signs of cramp.

When that set in, he could expect a whole heap more punishment.

As it was, he could well be dead before Rip Ohlrig called a halt to the mad ride deep into the desert south of the low-slung Brazos Breaks.

He had expected at least another brutal beating from Ohlrig after they had dragged him out of the river, but apart from the odd kick in the belly the ramrod hadn't harmed him. It was on Kent's orders and this puzzled Fargo. He could see by the set of Mickey Gann's weathered features that he, too, was puzzled why the rancher didn't either put a bullet in Fargo or beat the living hell out of him.

But Kent Rockwell had been relaxed, smiling, even content that he had Fargo in his hands once more. He sat on a rock while the young wrangler lay there in his wet and muddy clothes, stripped of his sixgun – somewhere he guessed he had lost Noble's Bowie knife. Kent lit up a cigarillo while Rip stood by expectantly.

'Gonna give you a chance, kid – aw, I ain't such a bad *hombre* that I want to kill my own blood-kin. No, don't figure I could live with that – I'll let nature do the job for me. You gotta die, you see that, don't you?'

'Because half the ranch is my legacy?'

Kent spread his hands. 'Well, that's how Brent planned it, but you see, *I'm* the one ran the whole she-bang while he was off buyin' cows and whorin' down in the border towns. *I did all the goddamn work!* And if you think I'm turnin' over half of what I built up to some punk-kid I don't even know, you got another think comin', feller! Fact is, I don't even know if you're who you say you are!'

'*You* said I was Gideon Rockwell,' gritted Fargo, and this time Kent walked forward and kicked him hard in the side. 'I just haven't had a chance to prove it yet, damn you!'

'And you won't! You set that son of a bitch Gabe Luckett on to my daughter. You ain't gonna get away with that! No matter who the hell you are.'

'Yeah, well, I'm sorry about that. Sam just figured it would be the quickest way to get your attention and put you in a position where you had to offer me a job. I didn't realize she was so young.'

Rockwell kicked him again. 'You're gonna die, kid! For that as much as anythin' else. It's gonna be slow and you're gonna have a lot of pain. I won't be there to see it but – like I said, you'll have your chance.' He laughed shortly. 'You get through alive and I reckon you'll have earned your share of Rockin' R . . . but the odds are pretty damn much agin that. I ain't worried you'll ever try to collect.'

Still smiling, he made a sign to Ohlrig and went back and sat on the low boulder.

With Mickey Gann helping – a little reluctantly, Fargo thought – Rip dropped his lasso loop over Fargo's head, pulled it tight around his chest, high up under his arms. Then he took a couple of turns around Fargo's arms while Gann held them, ran the rope to his saddlehorn and climbed up on to the horse, looking at Kent Rockwell for the signal to start.

'Go with Rip, Mickey,' Kent said, and the wrangler snapped his head around, shocked.

'Me? I don't want nothin' to do with this, boss!'

'You've already had plenty to do with it,' snapped Kent. 'Go with Rip, damn you!'

'I don't need him,' Ohlrig said, but Kent glowered.

'Take him along. We involve him and he daren't

open his mouth.'

'Hell, I wouldn't say nothin'!' Mickey assured the rancher but Rockwell scowled and jerked his head at Rip.

'Mount up, Mickey!' the ramrod yelled, and Gann slowly climbed aboard his horse, looking worried.

Fargo was struggling against the rope but Rip held it taut and when Gann settled into leather he jammed home the spurs and his mount snorted and lunged forward, almost dislocating Fargo's shoulders.

The desert started several hundred yards away and by the time he felt the hot, abradant sand and alkali tearing at his clothes, Fargo was already bleeding from several places where his body had been carelessly bounced off rocks and rough patches. Several times he tried to stay on his feet, but he stumbled after a dozen yards and sprawled flat again.

Now they were far out into the desert and his shirt was mostly gone, the knees of his pants were worn through and the toes of his boots were thinning at an alarming rate. Occasionally he glimpsed Mickey Gann riding alongside, but mostly any view he had was obscured by the thudding hoofs of Rip Ohlrig's horse and the dust and grit and clods they kicked up.

He wasn't fully conscious and his mind wandered and he allowed it to travel far from his present predicament, down through the years he had spent with the Comanche. The first tribe he had been with wandered far and were often in the Brazos Breaks, but they had been virtually wiped out in a cavalry raid and the survivors taken to the Falcone Reservation in the San

Marcos country near the Edwards Plateau. The chief's name had been Black Storm, but he hadn't lived up to his name and was soon ousted by his own brother, Bloody Lance. This man had traded Fargo, then known as White Reed because of his leanness, with another white boy who had later died, to a tribe whose country was far to the north. Only later when he began to grow to his full height and he looked into himself and saw a vision of an eagle and a wolf was he renamed Tall Wolf: some Indians changed their names with each new season throughout their lifetime.

They were good days, although he had to endure an occasional beating by those of the squaws who hated anyone with white blood, women who had lost their men to the whites.

He allowed his mind to gather details of the fishing and swimming expeditions with the boys, the tutoring by the warriors in the Indian lifestyle, the rough games that were devised to teach them how to fight – and to survive.

These things occupied the focus of his mind and he did not feel most of the pain racking his bouncing body and he was surprised when Rip Ohlrig slowed down, but it was only to rest the horse and give it a hatful of water from the big saddle canteen. There was no water for Fargo.

Then they started forward again, and through the dust cloud he saw the sun beginning its slide into the west. The heat was sapping his strength and he didn't know how much longer he could hold the bar-taut rope. His hands were already blistered but the

Comanche had taught him to ignore pain. Even so, his hands were giving him a lot of agony, bones were aching, muscles felt torn and strained and cramped. His body was being hammered by the earth and his lungs choked with dust and clogged with alkali. His senses were spinning and he fought to get his mind focused again on a time and place far from here and had just about managed it when they stopped abruptly.

He collapsed, his face pressing into the hot, fine sand. He coughed and choked and felt the rope slacken.

Fargo rolled on to his side and Rip Ohlrig shook loose the coils and slipped the loop from around his chest which was rubbed raw in a deep stinging groove. Rip smiled crookedly as Fargo blinked rapidly, trying to clear grit from his eyes by making tears flow.

'You're in better shape than I figured you'd be, Injun – but that don't count for much in the desert. Say, can't leave you any water or grub or weapons, but how'd you like a little company?'

Fargo frowned, gasping and coughing. He saw Rip's sixgun come up and suddenly Mickey Gann was yelling, trying to wrench his horse's head around, raking with his spurs. But he was way too late.

Rip shot him out of the saddle, one bullet hammering the wrangler to the ground, the second knocking him over on to his face. Stunned, Fargo watched as Rip squatted beside the older man, went through his pockets, sorting out what he wanted, discarding the rest – including the silver dollar with the Rocking R cut into it. Gann had taken it from Fargo's pockets before he had been roped-up behind the ramrod's horse. Rip apparently had no interest in it.

Ohlrig stood, grinning down at Fargo. 'Not much to show for thirty-forty years of work, huh?' But he put the few pathetic belongings into his pockets, staring down at Fargo all the time.

'Why?' Fargo croaked, rolling his eyes towards the wrangler's body.

Ohlrig shrugged. 'Knew too much, I guess. Kent din' want to risk him shootin' off his mouth after takin' on a load of likker. Well, you got a nice cool evenin' comin' your way, feller. Enjoy it – because tomorrow you're gonna find out what hell is like!' He grinned. 'Bad place, this desert, ain't it?' He leaned over Fargo. 'Hope it kills you slow and painful!'

Whistling, he mounted after taking Gann's guns and the wrangler's hat. Fargo's hat had been lost earlier at the river. Then Rip spat on Fargo, and rode back the way he had come, leading Gann's mount.

In minutes, the only sound was the wind blowing sand and grit across the miles of empty desolation stretching away to the horizon on all sides.

From now until he died, this would be Fargo's world.

His clothes were in shreds but while Micky Gann was a much smaller man, he could still make use of some of the old wrangler's bloodstained clothing.

When he got painfully to his feet, groaning involuntarily, he found his balance was out of kilter and he dropped to his knees, leaned gently forward on to his hands and stayed that way for a long time, head hanging, ears buzzing, the world spinning crazily. Gradually, it settled down to an even keel and he crawled over beside Gann's huddled form.

He found the silver dollar that Rip Ohlrig had discarded with such disdain. Now he saw why. It was bent and misshapen – apparently it had been in Gann's shirt pocket and one of Rip's bullets had hit it, distorting the metal. The Rocking R brand was still clearly legible on the back. He slipped it into the one remaining pocket of his torn trousers and leaned over Gann.

He jumped back as the wrangler suddenly coughed and flopped over on to his back. The man's sand-dusted eyelids flickered open and he stared around him at the sun-hammered sky. He coughed again and one hand crawled feebly across his body to the bleeding bullet wound high on the left side of his chest. On the right side, a little lower down, there was a dark bruise the size of a man's open hand and a trickle of blood where the edge of the coin had torn the flesh.

'You've got the luck of the Irish, Mickey,' Fargo said hoarsely.

Gann's dulled eyes rolled down to look at him. 'Some luck,' he whispered. 'Left for dead . . . out . . . here with . . . you. . . . Got any water?'

'What we've got is what we're wearing, Mickey. Nothing else.'

Mickey started to cuss Ohlrig, but he was too weak to make much of an effort.

Fargo told him how the coin had likely saved his life. 'The other wound's pretty deep, I guess the bullet's still in there.'

'What . . happens . . . now?'

Fargo squinted against the sinking sun's glowing disc. 'We're a long ways from anywhere, Mickey. We better get what sleep we can tonight. . . . It's gonna be hell tomorrow.'

He tore off some of the remains of his shirt, twisted it, ripped the pocket from Gann's shirt and used it as a wad, tying it over the wound. Gann passed out with the pair, and when he came round again, the first stars were out and he was bitching so bad that Fargo threatened if he didn't shut up he'd fill his mouth with sand, still hot from the day's sun.

'Judas, Fargo, don't – don't leave me here to die . . . all alone . . . with the flies and maggots feedin' on me! I-I can't stand the thought of that!'

'Mightn't have any choice, Mickey.'

Fargo examined the bullet wound. The pad was soaked with blood but he thought the bleeding had eased some, the clothing making a seal as the blood congealed. Then he began to scrape a hollow in the sand, stopping frequently because his hands and wrists were raw from the ropes. When he had it deep enough he dragged Gann into the trench and the wrangler thrashed in painful protest. 'Christ! Don't bury me!'

Fargo began to scoop sand back over him in a thin. layer. 'Gets mighty cold out here at night, Mickey. The sand'll keep you warm.'

He began digging a trench for himself to lie in, Gann watching in silence.

Fargo grunted, sucked in a sharp breath as he pulled

the sand over his tortured body, the alkali biting like hot coals into his raw flesh.

Tomorrow, he knew, the sun would flay him.

'Mickey, I'm gonna have to leave you here.'

The terrifying words probed into Gann's fevered brain and he wrenched his head around, still partly covered by the sand, one arm exposed. '*No!*'

Gann's sandy face was already burning, partly from growing fever, partly from the sun just becoming visible above the horizon.

'You gotta take me with you. I-I can tell what I know – how Kent killed your father—'

'Thanks, Mickey – but none of that matters now.'

'Where you . . . goin'? You know this desert. . . ?'

'I've been here before – long time ago. I was just a kid.'

'You recollect which way . . . to-to go?'

'I watched the stars last night – I think I can figure the direction. There used to be an old Indian well somewhere out there, if I'm right.'

'Christ! Take me with you, Fargo! Please!'

'Can't, Mickey. But I'll come back for you if I can.'

Then Fargo groped through the sand and, against startled protests and curses, pulled down Gann's trousers.

'The *hell* are you *doin'*? You gone plumb loco?'

Fargo rigged the worn trousers in a kind of tent, over Mickey's head, holding the edges down with sand scooped on to the legs, propping the body part into an inverted *V* with two dead sticks. Then he eased off

Gann's shirt but the pain caused the man to pass out.

When he came round, his body was covered with a layer of sand again but his face and head were shaded with the trousers. He looked to the right and saw nothing but heat-pulsing, empty desert. The same when he turned to the left – and he felt the panic set his heart pounding wildly. He lifted his head a little, looked along the low hump that marked his body and beyond his feet he saw a tall figure staggering away into the blistering sunlight, tracks wavering like those of a giant snake. Fargo had Gann's bloody shirt wrapped around his head.

Gann tried to call out, but already thirst was closing his throat.

Then Mickey Gann began to cry, surprised there was enough moisture left in his racked frame to produce tears.

The anguished sounds were instantly swallowed up by the enormous red-and-grey silence of the desert.

The first day was the worst.

Heat and dehydration, the raw ropeburns starting to dry and crack and ooze a clear fluid. Soon they would fester. Somehow, flies were conjured up out of nowhere and their persistence made him want to scream. They infested his nostrils, his eyes, the corners of his mouth, and fed ravenously on his wounds.

Fargo's tongue was rough and swollen, seeming to fill his mouth. His breath came in ragged gasps, his nostrils feeling as if hot pokers had been pushed up them. The glare nearly blinded him.

But next morning, crawling stiffly and weakly out of the shallow grave that had been his bed, he saw a darker smudge in the sand that a hot wind blew in a low, brownish mist just above the surface of the desert: wind the Indians called 'The Breath Of The Grey One' – synonymous with death.

He crawled towards the dark patch, wincing at the scraping of the sand against his raw kneecaps. It was the remains of a long-buried camp-fire and the very smallness of it told him it had been an Indian camp-fire. Only whitemen built huge blazing beacons just to cook the evening meal.

There were some small pieces of charcoal amongst the remains and he crushed some in his mouth, working up a little saliva, It tasted foul and gritty. He smeared the black mess under his eyes, around the sockets and down his peeling nose.

Immediately he felt relief from the burning irritation of glare that had previously reflected off his cheekbones and nose into his eyes. The black smudge dulled this way down.

The long-dead fire also told him that he was travelling an unseen trail that had been travelled before, probably for many years, by Indians crossing the desert.

But would it lead to the well he vaguely remembered?' Or was it just an invisible trail to Eternity. . . ?

Although it seemed to be a featureless landscape the Indians who travelled this desert – Comanche, Apaches, Kiowa and even Caddo at times – would have marked *something* that would lead them to water if they came this way again. It was how they survived.

He looked about him, eyes shaded a little by the bulge of Gann's shirt wrapped turban-like around his head. Even so, his brain felt as if the cushioning water protecting it inside his skull was ready to boil. There was nothing that he would call a landmark, not by the wildest stretch of his imagination. Just a vast empty wasteland.

Beckoning. . . .

But there was no choice: he had to keep moving.

He slogged on, legs weakening with each step, tongue beginning to protrude from between his scaling lips now: he felt the hot wind on its tip, like acid dripping on to the flesh.

His belly growled and he pushed aside thoughts of hunger. But it was not so easy trying to forget his raging thirst. His pain-racked body cried out for moisture. He tumbled down a small slope and felt disoriented when he pushed to his feet, looking for the sun.

His brain thudded like a drum inside his skull.

He had no idea where he was or how much time had passed, but some time later he realized that the sun was well past the meridian and beginning the long daily fall into the west. Much of the time he spent on hands and knees now, muttering to himself, mostly gibberish. He cussed Kent Rockwell with a stream of oaths. Another time he framed an apology to Liza Rockwell for having set Gabe Luckett on to her. . . .

Most of the time, he didn't know what he was doing. He even began to hallucinate. He fell, sprawling, hot sand filling his mouth, the flies buzzing and crawling.

Some time later he felt a slight trembling through

his body like muted thunder. Then it stopped. The following silence was broken by a *zipping!* sound. He was too tired to lift his head to see what had caused it.

But eventually he did and blinked as the object half-buried in the sand in front of his face came into focus.

An Ash arrow-shaft, fletched with feathers of the desert eagle in the Comanche manner.

10
Second Chance

Kent Rockwell felt that there had been a heavy weight lifted from his shoulders.

It was over a week now since Ohlrig had taken Fargo and Gann into the desert. There had been reports of a bad sandstorm out there – the two bodies would be buried under feet of shifting sand by now. *Things were looking up!* He had gotten rid of his worries in one hit – Mickey Gann because Kent had always figured Gann knew too much about brother Brent's death.

And as for that son of a bitch, 'Lee Fargo' – Kent's guts had churned into mush the moment Rip Ohlrig had brought in the marked silver dollar he had found in Fargo's warbag. He had recognized it as the one he had seen Brent make years ago, ready to hang around his baby's neck. 'To mark his legacy,' Brent had said. Kent had never seen the kid and never thought he would. He was a hard, ruthless man, but something deep inside him made him balk when it came to harming – all right, *murdering* – a child. Especially one that had Rockwell blood in his veins.

Brent – well, the hatred between the Rockwell brothers had been there all their lives. Kent always figured Brent had had the better deal. Tall and handsome, he was always his parents' favourite. His father had shown his trust in Brent by readily settling more and more responsibility on him as he grew older, praising him for his efforts to cope. While he, Kent, was criticized and whipped and cussed for not doing his chores properly. The old man had actually told him once, '*You'll never be half the man Brent is. Never!*'

A hard thing for a man to live with. Brent had tried to keep things friendly, but Kent would have none of it. He felt despised and useless even though he busted his back trying to please, and was truly surprised when the old man died and cut him in for a share of the spread – twenty-five per cent against Brent's seventy-five. Still, it was more than Kent had expected – though sure not anywhere near as much as he *wanted – or figured he had earned.*

It was the old man's wish that they would, in turn, pass it along to their offspring. That way the Rockwell name would be perpetuated.

Well, that was as maybe, but Kent had made up his mind a long time ago that *his* offspring were going to be the only ones to inherit Rocking R. Then, without a word, Brent had gone and got himself married to some damn Mex woman while away on one of his many cattle-buying trips – while Kent slaved and sweated and worried back on the Rocking R. And later had sprung it on him that he had a son – and *heir*! – just waiting in the wings. Kent had harboured the notion all his life that he had been treated like dirt by the rest of the family and as far as he was concerned here was just another example of it.

Brent had started to give him some stupid explanation about knowing how Kent disliked Mexicans (*hated* them would be closer to the truth) and so he had put off telling him until he had to. Rosa, his 'wife' – Kent always thought of her with a sneer although he had never met the woman – *and* didn't want to come to that! – had been caring for her ailing mother for years and now the old woman had finally died and Rosa had to get out of the house in the small village where she and the kid had been living. So it was time to bring her to her real home – the Rocking R.

'Kent, it's gonna be real good havin' 'em around here . . . you'll see.'

'*Like hell I will!*'

Kent had walked out at that point and Brent had run after him, grabbed him by the arm, getting rough. The big argument had started then and Brent had hammered Kent brutally, stood over him, and said between gritted teeth in that scary way he had when he meant something with all his heart – and didn't aim to let anything turn him from it, 'You always were a whinin' little bastard! Now get this – I'm bringing Rosa and Gideon to Rockin' R whether you like it or not. They'll move into their own quarters and you'll treat 'em with respect and consideration. Or, little brother, you're gonna need a helluva lot of dental work and you'll be wearin' your nose on the wrong side of your head!'

It had scared Kent as Brent's anger had always scared him, because Brent was just like the old man, in looks and temperament, even in the sound of his voice. His whole body cringed at such times as he faced Brent's anger – but this time, there was the whole spread at stake as far as Kent was concerned. No damn Mexican, or kid with Mex blood in his veins, was going to get his hands on any part of Rocking R!

Not while he could prevent it.

It took him a little time to realize just what had to be done – and how to go about it. . . .

He lost a deal of sleep worrying about the boy, though. The Mex woman – well, he could live with that, but the boy, not much more than a baby – something rebelled inside him. *That* was when he remembered Sam Noble.

It was time for that hell-raiser to square his debts.

But, old Sam had let him down, gone chicken-livered and lied about having killed Rosa and Gideon. No longer mattered, of course. The Lucketts had taken care of Noble and Rip had finally taken care of Gideon – and Mickey Gann who may or may not have been a danger. *Better safe than sorry.*

So, for now, he had no worries, only the running of the spread and the running *off* of those sod-busters down along Eliza Creek named after his mother. *She* had drowned there a long time ago and sometimes he thought his father had driven her to it, although no one had ever suggested she had taken her own life. . . .

*

Kent glanced up now as the door opened and Rip Ohlrig, dust-spattered and sweaty from ranch chores, came in rolling a cigarette.

'Panhandle said you wanted to see me.' He dropped into a chair without invitation.

Kent scowled but only said, 'Take ten of the boys tonight and clear Eliza Creek.'

Licking the cigarette paper, Rip looked up sharply.
'All of it?'

'The whole she-bang! I'm fed up to the teeth seein' them sod-busters and their dirt-roofed huts and slat-ternly womenfolk and snotty-nosed kids foulin' up that creek. Drive 'em out, burn 'em out. Do whatever you have to, but make sure they get the message – they're finished here.'

Rip slowly lit his cigarette, blew smoke at the ceiling, stained a deep mellow gold from many years of tobacco fumes. 'Finally makin' your move, huh?'

'It's time I got Rockin' R back to its original size. *That's* how I aim to pass it along to Liza. It's *her* inheritance and I owe it to her to make sure it's all it should be.'

Rip picked a tobacco flake from the tip of his tongue. 'That "bonus" you promised me for doin' the desert chore – it don't really cover a raid on the sod-busters, too.'

Kent curled a lip. 'You're a greedy son of a bitch, Rip, but you give good value for money. So, OK, I'll pay you fightin' wages for the raid. Throw a couple of extra dollars into the pockets of every man you take with you and who comes back.'

Rip Ohlrig smiled slowly. 'Suits me.' He twisted the smile and threw Kent a mocking, sidelong look, adding, 'Goddamn Injuns!'

Both men laughed, enjoying the joke.

Whatever it was.

Pa Emmett was the first to die in the attack on his sod-roofed shack, built not ten yards away from the north bank of Eliza Creek.

He was foolish enough to poke his head out of one of the window gaps – no glass, only roughly constructed wooden slat panels that could be slipped in when the weather required it. They certainly weren't heavy enough to stop an arrow, let alone a bullet. But it was a bullet that found Pa's head and his skinny body was hurled back across the single room of the dirt-floored shack, shattered skull spilling its contents along the way. His wife screamed and was sick. The two girls, one eleven, the other thirteen, stared in horror at the thing that had once been a loving parent. Then they picked up the old percussion pistols they had been using, poked them through knotholes in the clapboards and pulled the triggers without aiming.

In the yard, the circling raiders howled and whooped and riddled the flimsy shack with bullets from repeating rifles. They circled ten times before the leader called a halt by lifting his right hand, a smoking Winchester rifle in his left.

Rip Ohlrig was barely recognizable as a whiteman in

his 'Indian' get-up: a pair of old trousers, dirt smeared all over his torso and arms and face, with stripes added in candleblack, a leather headband with a handful of feathers stuck in the back. He even had two lengths of plaited black-dyed rope dangling from the headband to make it look like his braided hair.

'Chick!' he called and another 'Indian' rode up alongside, dressed exactly like Rip. He had a short Comanche flatbow and a quiverful of arrows strapped to his saddle.

'Shoot off half-a-dozen arrows into the house and corral poles or the barn. Fire the buildings and drop a couple of feathers. We're movin' on to the Hallam place. Meet us over there.'

Chick nodded and quickly nocked an arrow to the bowstring, sending the shaft thudding into the door of the Emmett shack. He shot off three more into the crude building.

He heard a groan or two from inside. But it didn't stop him pouring coal oil over the building and setting it alight. When it was burning well, along with the three-sided barn and the corrals, he turned loose the two work mules and the buggy team, then rode away in the direction Rip Ohlrig had led his band of raiders.

Once he was away from the crackling of the fire, he could hear the distant rifle shots as Rip and his men shot up the Hallam place. After that would be the McLeods and that loner just setting up near Turpentine Bend, feller name of Chase, or Chance, something like that.

Not that it mattered. He would be dead before sun-up.

Then any other sod-buster with notions of settling along Eliza Creek ought to think twice before trying.

They'd have to be real dumb not to get tonight's message.

Lee Fargo crouched just inside the entrance flap of the sunlit tipi, straining to hear what the young army lieutenant was saying to Chief Rumpled Hair.

'Something about an Indian raid on the squatters along Eliza Creek,' Fargo reported quietly to Mickey Gann, who was propped up on a pile of buffalo robes, crude bandages spotted with blood about his chest. 'A lot of 'em were killed and they seem to be blaming Rumpled Hair.'

'When did it happen?' Gann's voice was weak and he spoke slowly. He looked pale and drawn, but was a long way better than when he had been brought in here from the desert with Fargo just over a week ago.

'Last night,' Fargo answered, signing to Gann to be quiet while he listened again. He swore softly. 'Rumpled Hair doesn't savvy enough English to know what the lieutenant's saying! He's nodding his head, the old fool!'

'Judas – if the army think he's admittin' to the raid, they'll turn this place into a butcher's shop. An' us with it!'

'Hell, he's all muddled!' Fargo straightened: he was wearing fringed buckskin trousers and an open decorated vest also with fringing. He had a beaded headband and the battered silver dollar hung around his neck. His body still showed healing scars and scabs from his rough drag across the desert at the end of Ohlrig's rope. He moved a little stiffly.

'I better go out there, Mickey.'

As he reached for the edge of the flap, Gann said sharply, 'Don't do it, Fargo! Judas, man, you go out there and word'll get back to Kent Rockwell about two wounded white men livin' with the Injuns! He'll know it has to be us! Or he'll come look to make sure! 'We gotta stay put!'

'Shut up, Mickey. These people saved our lives!' Fargo told him in a quiet but hard voice. 'We can't let them be blamed for this when we can help them.'

'No, don't. . . ! Aw, *hell*!'

Gann was gasping for breath with his efforts and emotion as Fargo ducked through the tipi entrance and crossed swiftly to where Chief Rumpled Hair and three of his old warriors stood facing the young lieutenant, a sergeant and two troopers. They watched Fargo approach and he lifted a hand.

'Lieutenant, couldn't help hearing – I've been here for more'n a week and I'll swear on a stack of Bibles that none of Rumpled Hair's men left this camp last night. These are all old men here. Old women, too, with just a couple of young squaws to help out. They're only interested in living the traditional way, and they have permits to stay outside the reservation; they could-n't mount a raid on a Sunday-school picnic, if they wanted to.'

The lieutenant was young, still with a pinkish bloom on his cheeks. He frowned and tried to look severe. The fact that he was at least six inches shorter than Fargo didn't help as he looked up into the sun-blistered and scarred face.

'And what're you doing here?' the officer snapped.

'These Comanche pulled me out of the desert after I was thrown and dragged by my horse. They saved my life.'

'So you're beholden to 'em!'

'I am, but I'm not lying. No one left this camp last night. Hell, they've only got a couple of old Sharps rifles and a Winchester with a loose lever anyway.'

The army officer signed to one of the troopers who held a grey blanket. The private unrolled it and spilled out ten or twelve broken arrows, a couple a little charred.

'These are Comanche arrows,' snapped the officer. 'Found at all four places that were raided last night.'

'They're not arrows of this tribe ... see? The forepart of the shaft is hardwood, the rest made of reeds. There are no reeds around here. This tribe uses ash or choke-cherry, tipped with flint, not iron like these.'

The lieutenant, who introduced himself as Doonan, ordered the two troopers to search the camp. Fargo told the old Comanche chief in his own language what was happening. Rumpled Hair grunted, used to the army's rough and arrogant treatment.

'We have been punished before for crimes we have not committed. What is it this time we have not done, but for which we will be punished?'

Surprisingly, Doonan flushed and did not answer. Fargo, for the first time, saw soldiers on the hillside, mounted, Trapdoor Springfield rifles at the ready.

'Your name, sir?' Doonan asked abruptly, a notebook out now, all business and very serious.

'Wolf,' Fargo told him. 'Mr Wolf.'

Doonan wrote dutifully, asked where he was from and why he had been in the desert. Fargo lied easily, not sure if the soldier believed him. Then the troopers returned with perhaps a hundred arrows, each one made from a length of ash or choke-cherry, tipped with a flint point. They were also crested with red, yellow and black paint in stripes and checks. The officer pursed his lips.

'These are hunting arrows, not for war, Lieutenant,' Fargo pointed out. 'The tips and paint tell you that.'

'He's right about the arrows, sir,' said the sergeant. 'And, fact is, all them sod-busters was shot to death. The guns we found here couldn't've done it. Too old an' not enough of 'em. You know I ain't no Injun-lover, sir, but—'

'Just *look* at these people, Lieutenant. Look how old they are. Look at their horses! Nothing here resembles a war party. Why don't you go ask Kent Rockwell about the raid?' Fargo said, his words bringing a frown to Doonan's face.

'Now just a minute! It was Rockwell's men who reported the raid.'

'I could be wrong, sure, but Rockwell has no use for sod-busters – even less for Indians. He wouldn't mind throwing the blame on to Rumpled Hair and his old warriors.'

'I have heard . . . rumours about Rockwell's – er –

roughshod methods, but tracks pointed in this general direction. Though my sergeant here did remark it was strange that the raiders had turned loose the farmers' livestock. Usually they take them away. . . .'

The man was wavering.

'Go ask Rockwell, Lieutenant.' Fargo could see Doonan was inexperienced, treading warily, not wanting to be the cause of any more wrongful Indian massacres after the outrage whipped up by the bloody, uncontrolled punitive raids in the wake of Custer's slaughter. Even a vengeful public had hollered 'Enough!'

Treatment of Indians was a political hot potato right now and any young lieutenant with ambition would be a fool to knowingly chance making any mistakes that could cost him his commission – and career.

Then there was a small commotion at the tipi from which Fargo had emerged and one of the troopers sent to look for arrows poked his head out of the entrance and called, 'There's another white man in here, Lieutenant! He's been shot,'

Doonan glanced sharply at Fargo then motioned to the sergeant. 'Keep an eye on Mr Wolf here while I have a few words with this other man . . . whom you seem to have forgotten to mention, Wolf! This is getting more interesting by the minute!'

Fargo went very still as the sergeant casually swung the barrel of his saddle carbine around to cover him.

He need not have worried – Gann played along.

But young Lieutenant Harrison Doonan was no fool. When he rode out to question Kent Rockwell, after

Gann – who gave his name as Charlie Michaels – backed up Fargo's story and said that Rockwell had been hacked by the sod-busters' presence for months, he left six soldiers armed with repeating rifles camped down by the Indian horses, just to make sure that the small group of Comanche would still be here when he returned – as well as Fargo and Gann. He didn't seem quite sure just what to make of them; their stories not only matched, but made sense.

However, the soldiers were no match for the guile and wiles of the two young squaws amongst Rumpled Hair's people. Acting coy and shyly giggling, they easily captivated the lonely, women-starved soldiers who were soon jostling each other for a turn at sampling the lithe young girls' charms. . . .

And while they did so, Fargo and Gann quit the camp with two of Rumpled Hair's best mustangs and with his blessing. Gann managed to steal one of the soldier's Winchesters and a bandolier of ammunition while the owner was kept busy by one of the squaws. Rumpled Hair gave Fargo his own personal osage-wood bow, backed with rattlesnake skin, and a cougar-skin quiver of twenty arrows. It was an important gesture of trust and respect.

'You are still Comanche, Tall Wolf, despite your skin,' the old chief said. 'Use the bow well.'

Fargo thanked Rumpled Hair. 'I won't forget what you have done for us.'

'For you – the other one you must watch closely.'

That was all the warning the Indian gave, but Fargo heeded it. Rumpled Hair was old – and a good judge of men.

*

They reined down on the ridge above the camp, Gann swaying in the saddle, still suffering from the bullet wound. Fargo was in much better shape but Gann had decided to come along, though reluctantly.

'Judas Priest, Fargo!' he had complained. 'There we were, safe from Kent and Rip Ohlrig, and you had to go spoil it by showin' yourself to that young shavetail!'

'Quit your griping, Mickey,' Fargo told him without sympathy. 'You wouldn't be alive now except for those Indians. They were going to be in a heap of trouble. We had to speak up.'

'Yeah – an' look where it's got us!'

'You're a real pain in the butt, Mickey. We've been given a second chance. Now make the most of it. I'm riding on at my own pace. If you can't keep up it'll be just too bad!'

'Hey, wait up! I-I'm comin'!' Gann rode up alongside Fargo. 'Where we goin', by the way?'

Fargo grinned tightly and there was just enough starlight for Gann to see his white teeth.

'Back to Rocking R – where else?'

11
Gold!

They had to rest. Gann couldn't stay in the saddle much longer so Fargo cut across to a draw that Gann directed him to. He helped the wounded man down from the saddle and propped him against a tree. Mickey nursed the rifle with a death-grip, only releasing it reluctantly so as to drink from the animal-bladder water bag Fargo offered him.

He swallowed but grimaced. 'Tastes like panther's piss!'

'Wouldn't know. Never tried it.' Fargo drank deeply.

'Hell, you're more Comanche than whiteman! Why the hell you got that bow and arrer?' He slapped the rifle breech. '*This* is what you need!'

'Got nothing against guns, but I grew up with bows and arrows, Mickey. Had my first one shoved into my hands when I was four years old and used one right up until Sam Noble took me away from the tribe.'

'Hell, guns is faster, more deadly. Din' you learn that much?'

'No. Seems that way to whites, I guess, but I can shoot off six arrows and hit my target faster than you or any white man can fire a revolver – I've done it many a time. *And* an arrow will penetrate more wood than a bullet.'

'Hogwash!'

'Fact, Mickey. Not the time to try and prove it, but I've seen it happen. Anyway, Rumpled Hair gave me his personal bow. It's a mark of respect and honour. I couldn't't've refused if I'd wanted to.'

'Well, if we run into any Rockin' R hands, you stay close to me – I know which weapon'll get us outa trouble!' He paused, breathless, rubbing at his bandaged wound. 'You ain't yet said why we're committin' suicide.'

Fargo smiled crookedly. 'By going back to Rocking R? There's something on Rockwell land I have to collect and take to San Antone.'

Gann shook his head, too weary to ask about details.

But he was wide awake when Fargo, using landmarks remembered from Noble's map, led the way into canyon country on the north-west side of Rocking R.

'Hell, what're we doin' here? Rockin' R use that canyon yonder, below the butte, for round-up. Kent had men workin' there last week.'

'We won't be long. Looking for a wall with a big slab of black rock in it.'

'I know the place, but ain't nothin' there. Wall's blank.'

'Let's go, Mickey.'

Reluctantly Gann led the way, plainly worried about

them being sighted by any Rocking R hands in the neighbouring canyon by the crumbling butte, less than a mile away.

'There it is – Black Face Canyon. Some of the mustangs used to come here for a spell but I trapped so many they moved on to that area we were workin' before all this trouble. This rock's solid, Fargo, what you want here?'

Fargo didn't answer, recalling once more what Noble had written on his map. He dismounted from the small wooden Indian saddle, let the hackamore trail, and walked to where the black rock made a sharp line as it slanted across the lighter-coloured sandstone. He lined himself up with this, walked north along the wall seven paces and came to a small clump of rocks. He unslung the bow and quiver of arrows he had worn across his back, stood them against the rockface.

Gann watched, puzzled, as Fargo heaved the rocks aside one by one, then picked up a dead stick and began probing the earth where they had lain. The stick only penetrated a few inches in one spot and he knelt, took out the hunting knife he wore on his rawhide belt and began to dig. It was an Indian blade, a trade knife, of inferior steel, and blunted and burred on the point even before he had opened up an area about a foot square.

He set the knife aside, scooped dirt out with his hands. Then he retrieved the first rawhide poke and set it on the edge of the hole. The rawhide had rotted in several places and, as he dug deeper, some small nuggets spilled out.

Fargo, removing three more drawstring bags, did not hear the sharp, hissing intake of breath from Gann as the wrangler recognized the gold for what it was. But he heard the click! made by the rifle hammer as Gann cocked the weapon.

'Now, what have we here?'

Fargo turned slowly, holding the last sagging bag of nuggets. He stared at Gann who seemed steady enough in the saddle now, a tight grin on his wrinkled face.

'Sam Noble's treasure?'

'Not his treasure – what he's prospected over the years. I promised to take it to his grandchildren in San Antone.'

'Hell, looks to be a goodly haul! But I heard, Sam panned the creeks around here and back in the hills over the years. Cunnin' ol' sonuver never once let slip he'd found any colour!'

'He was stashing it away for his grandkids . . . you gonna put down that gun, Mickey?'

'Well, I dunno – I mean, his grandkids won't miss it will they, because they've never had it. But you an' me, Fargo, we've been whupped and shot and stampeded over. You ask me, we've *earned* a whole heap more'n we've gotten lately.'

Fargo continued to stare and those chill blue eyes made Gann squirm a little. He tightened his grip on his rifle and it seemed to give him more confidence: after all, he had the drop here.

'I gave my word, Mickey.'

'Sam was a no-good sidewinder. He was an outlaw when Kent took him in. A murderer.'

'He could've been cleared, but Kent kept him on a string for his own use, blackmailing him into doing dirty chores for him. But that makes no nevermind, what he was. He saved my neck by getting me away from the Comanche before the army massacre. I owe him my life and he headed me in the direction of a legacy I didn't know about. But it all gets down to one thing, Mick – *I gave my word.*'

Gann frowned. 'Every Injun I ever knowed never bothered none about keepin' his word to a whiteman!'

'You didn't see their best side, Mickey – they never showed that to the whiteman. Now, put up the gun.'

Gann shook his head. 'Don't reckon I will. You don't want to share that gold with me, why, I reckon I might as well take the lot. I din' give *my* word to nobody!'

He lifted the rifle towards his right shoulder and his face was pulled out of shape briefly by the spasm of pain it caused him. He gasped, hesitating, and Fargo hurled the small bag of gold. It struck Gann high in the chest, beside his wound, and he yelled as he tumbled from the saddle. The rifle exploded, the bullet laying a bright silver streak across the black-faced rock before ricocheting spitefully.

By the time the dazed wrangler picked himself up, only managing to reach a sitting position against the rockface, Fargo had him covered with drawn bow, the flint arrowhead aimed squarely at Gann's chest.

Mickey paled and lifted one hand. The other was pressed against his chest wound which was bleeding now. 'Don't Fargo! I-I was only joshin'!'

'Sure you were, Mickey,' Fargo said, eyes narrowed.

He did not lower the bow as he used his moccasined foot to draw the six bags of gold nuggets into a pile. 'Another advantage the bow has over a gun is silence. If Kent has men working that other canyon they'll have heard your shot.'

'Hell, yeah! C'mon! Gimme a hand up. We gotta get outa here!'

'Not *we*, Mick – you stay. I can't trust you no matter what. Now just shut up your whining! You brought this on yourself. Here – you want some gold?'

He reached down and picked up two nuggets about the size of his thumbnail that had spilled from the rotted bag, tossing them into Gann's lap.

'See if it'll buy your way out of trouble.'

He replaced his arrow in the quiver, slung it on to his back and the bow across his chest. He scooped up the bags of gold, dropping another two small nuggets, but leaving them lie. He stowed the drawstring pokes in the buckskin bag slung from the Indian saddle, then scooped up Gann's rifle and the pouch of cartridges.

'Hey! I need protection!' whined Gann.

Fargo mounted and rode away without replying. Gann called after him but he didn't look round. . . .

Twenty minutes later, three sweat-reeking cowboys riding Rocking R mounts, and carrying guns in their hands, found Gann beside the hole dug by Fargo. He had scratched up one more nugget from the raw earth and was holding it in his hand as the cowpokes walked across, guns menacing.

'Well, I reckon the boss'll be glad to see you!' Chick Sawtell allowed.

*

Kent Rockwell snapped his head around in a savage, raw glare at Rip Ohlrig.

'By God, looks like the only way to be sure of things is for me to do my own killin'!'

Ohlrig's jaws were clamped, bunches of knotted muscle showing, and his big brutal fists clenched tightly as he looked at Mickey Gann sprawled on the ground at the foot of the ranch-house steps in the yard of the Rocking R.

The ramrod snapped his gaze to Chick Sawtell. 'You done right bringin' him in, Chick. Now, go on back to the round-up.'

Chick nodded, but looked at Rockwell and the rancher made a 'Get out of here!' gesture and the cowboy strode back to his horse and rode out. By then, Gann was sitting up, shirt front stained with fresh blood. Rip walked over and thrust a boot against his shoulder, knocking the man on to his back, pinning him there with the same boot.

'Where's Fargo?'

Gann shook his head. 'D-dunno, Rip – gospel!'

Rip glanced at Rockwell who nodded and then watched dispassionately as Ohlrig did the work he loved the best.

Kent's face was impassive, but inside he was churning. Had been so since that shavetail lieutenant had ridden in and started questioning him about the raid on the sod-busters. The man had pulled him up by the short hairs, though, when he had mentioned the two wounded white men at the Indian camp. Especially one wearing a mangled silver dollar around his neck.

He thought he had convinced Doonan that he had had nothing to do with the raid on Eliza Creek – though he wasn't certain-sure; that young officer just might be a lot smarter than he let on – and he had been about to ride out to the damn Comanche camp and see for himself if the men were Gann and Fargo.

Then Chick had dragged in Mickey Gann.

And now the man lay bloody and unconscious while Rip knelt beside him and went through his pockets. Looking surprised, he held out his hand where the four nuggets of gold now glittered in the midday sun.

Rockwell frowned down at them. 'Bring him round.'

Rip did this by the simple matter of scooping up a pail of water from the nearby horsetrough and tossing it over the wounded man. Gann spluttered and coughed, snatching at his chest. Terror showed on his face as he realized where he was and saw the gold in Rockwell's hand.

'Where'd this come from?'

Gann swallowed. *Mebbe there was a way out of this yet.* 'Fargo dug it up. Black Face Canyon. Said it was Sam Noble's. Had six pokes of-of nuggets. . . .'

Rip arched his eyebrows and Rockwell's face showed greed. 'On my land!'

'Dunno if . . . Sam got it . . . in the canyon, boss, but he sure . . . buried it there. For-for his grandkids – 'cordin' to Fargo.'

Rockwell glowered at Ohlrig. 'Christ I oughta kill *you*, Rip!'

'I dunno how either of 'em lived.' Ohlrig kicked Gann in the ribs, shaking him when the man sobbed in pain. 'How come you got outa that desert?'

'The Injuns. Knew Fargo. Took us . . . to their . . . camp an' . . . fixed us up. . . .'

Rip cussed foully, surprising even Rockwell at one stage: the rancher thought he had heard every kind of oath there was but his ramrod pulled a couple out of the hat that were new to him. Not that any of them did any good. . . .

'Where's Fargo?' Rockwell's voice was deceptively quiet and without edge as he looked down at Gann. 'C'mon, Mickey. He run out and left you – why protect him?'

Gann's face was pathetic as he raised it to look at the rancher. 'If I-I tell you . . . will you lemme go?'

Rockwell spread his hands out from his side. 'Hell, why not? I don't need you, Mickey. All I want is Fargo.'

'But you had Rip try to shoot me.'

'We-ell – just thought you knew too much. But you've proved you can keep your mouth shut. You never told that shavetail anythin', did you?'

Gann's battered face brightened slightly. 'No! That's right, boss, I can keep my mouth shut.'

'Yeah, I know that now, Mickey. So where's Fargo?'

Gann hesitated and Rip growled, made a menacing move towards him and Gann, flinching at the thought of more pain at the brutal ramrod's hands, said, 'He's took the gold to Noble's grandkids.'

'*Where*, for Chris'sakes?' snapped Ohlrig.

Mickey threw an arm across his eyes. 'San-San Antone! I swear. . . .'

Ohlrig looked quizzically at Rockwell who nodded slowly. 'Yeah, I think Mickey's speakin' gospel, Rip. I recollect Sam speakin' about his wife livin' there. She cleared out to some kinfolk after he turned outlaw.'

'I swear on my mother's grave, boss!' Gann said breathlessly.

'OK, Mickey, you did good.' He started to walk away towards the corrals.

'Where . . . where you goin'?' Gann croaked.

'Gonna arrange for some horses and packs for me and Rip. Long ride to San Antone.'

'What . . . what about me?' Gann's eyes were rolling worriedly in his head, but he relaxed some when Rockwell smiled.

'Rip'll help you on your way, Mickey.' The rancher flicked his gaze to the ramrod. 'Won't you, Rip?'

Ohlrig bared his teeth in a tight smile.

'Be a pleasure, boss.'

Then he took out his sixgun and the roar of the shot drowned Mickey Gann's scream.

12

Hope

Lee Fargo hardly resembled the white Indian who had left Mickey Gann in Black Face Canyon when he stepped down from the train at the San Antonio depot.

He wore a check shirt with a buckskin vest over it, decorated down the front with three silver conchos a side, from the centre of which dangled split buckskin thongs. His trousers were charcoal-grey cord with a dark stripe, tucked into the tops of plain leather half-boots. Around his waist he wore a second-hand gun rig – Colt Frontier model sixgun in a plain El Paso holster, the belt's bullet-loops filled with 44.40 shells that would fit both the Colt and the Winchester rifle Gann had stolen from the soldier at the Indian camp.

The rifle had been slipped beneath the straps of the warbag he now carried on his left shoulder as he walked up to the Plaza del Sol, sought and found the law office shingle and entered the dim coolness of the adobe building.

The man behind the desk was mid-forties, balding, wore a tobacco-stained frontier moustache and looked at him with hard, searching eyes. But he nodded civilly enough.

'Howdy. And what can I do for you so early this fine Texas morning?'

'Just came in on the train. Looking for a brother and sister name of Preston – Kyle and Jo – Josephine, I guess.'

'Uh-huh – and what would you be wanting with the Prestons?' The tone was casual but those eyes had narrowed a little.

'Got some business with 'em.'

'What kind?'

'Private.'

The sheriff arched his eyebrows. 'You being ornery?'

'No. Their grandfather died a little while back. Out on the Brazos – I was with him at the time and he asked me to deliver a parcel to the Prestons. I'm here to do just that.'

The lawman sighed. 'I guess I won't bother asking what's in the parcel—'

'I don't know,' lied Fargo easily.'I never opened it.'

The sheriff smiled thinly. 'Yeah – I'm the uncurious type myself. Your name is. . . ?'

'Lee Fargo – I'm a bronc-buster. Been working the Brazos.'

'Now you got new clothes, a pocketful of dinero and aim to cut loose the curly wolf after you deliver your parcel, right?'

Fargo sighed.

'I doubt there'll be time. It's taking me so long to find out where the Prestons live.'

The sheriff stood slowly, his gaze never moving from Fargo. He tapped his fingers against the desk edge. 'You'd best savvy this, mister – this town is kind of partial to the Prestons. They're young people who've had it mighty rough. Now you're bringing 'em more bad news about their grandpa – that and the parcel, whatever it is. If that's *all* you're bringing 'em, fine, but if there's any notion of making any kind of trouble for 'em . . . well, you'll soon find out it's the biggest mistake you ever made.'

'Hell, Sheriff, no need for this. I aim to deliver the parcel, answer any questions I can about the old feller and then be on my way. I've got no gripe with the Prestons. Don't even know 'em. Just gave my word to their granddad and I'm trying to keep it – if I ever get to 'em.'

'All right, all right – but you've been warned. You cross the plaza and go down Mission Street. All the way to the end. You'll see Kyle's shingle swinging above a gate – he works out of his house.'

'Shingle?'

'Kyle's an attorney. Struggling, but he shows promise and folk hereabouts throw whatever jobs they can his way.'

'You mean, *easy* jobs?'

The lawman shrugged. 'Like I said – struggling. You don't trust a sawbones straight out of medical school to cut open your wife, do you? You wait till he gets a little more experience.'

That was enough philosophy for Fargo right now and he took his leave, followed the sheriff's directions, and fifteen minutes later was shaking hands with Kyle and Jo Preston in the parlour of the old clapboard house at the end of Mission Street. There were only vacant lots beyond.

They were bright young people, resembled each other facially quite strongly, and made him feel welcome. Jo, a young woman about twenty, with golden, shoulder-length hair, said she would make coffee and went out of the room. Kyle was a little older, dressed formally in frockcoat and plain vest, over a white shirt with a four-in-hand blackstring tie at the throat. His trousers were neatly creased, pearl-grey. His face was open, his long fair hair brushed back in natural waves. Regulation legal attire.

But he was more natural and friendly than any attorney-at-law that Fargo had ever met, although he had to admit his experience of such people was pretty well limited. Kyle gestured to the sofa and Fargo sat down, unstrapped his warbag and opened it, taking out the parcel he had made of the gold nuggets. He handed it to Kyle who was startled by its weight, but asked, 'Is that an Indian bow and a set of arrows I see poking out of your bag?'

Fargo nodded. 'Comanche. It was a present. Old Sam got that parcel together over the years. He was a tough old bird, but his heart was in the right place, I guess.'

'We never knew him – we were told he was dead years ago.'

'He was just used to living alone, I guess. Felt kind of guilty he hadn't done anything for you before. There's an IOU in there, by the way – for a hundred and twelve dollars and forty-nine cents – I had to use that money to outfit myself and pay for stage and train fares. You'll get it back.'

Kyle seemed bewildered and Jo came in and set down tray with cups and coffee pot on a small table. Kyle opened the parcel and Jo gasped when the sunlight slanting through the window blazed on the small pile of gold nuggets.

'Why, there must be at least a thousand dollar there!' the girl said, turning her big hazel eyes on Fargo.

'I guess,' he said. 'Less what I had to use.'

The girl glanced at the IOU with his large, childish writing and signature. She smiled suddenly. 'You seem to be an honest man, Mr Fargo. You borrow from the gold and leave your note on it, and deliver the rest. You could have gone off with the lot and we'd've been none the wiser.'

An echo of Mickey Gann's words there. . . .

'I gave my word, ma'am,' he told her stiffly and she realized she had offended him when no offence had been meant.

'Sis means it's nice to find a truly honest man, Lee,' Kyle said quickly, trying to make amends as the girl poured coffee now. 'Can you tell us anything about Granddad? We really know very little except he was an army scout and mountain man.'

You won't find out about his outlaw days from me.

Aloud, after accepting the cup of coffee and fresh-baked biscuit from Jo, Fargo told them what he knew about Sam'l Houston Noble. He had to go back a way and explain how he came to be living with the Indians but he let them think Rockwell had left him in the wilderness to be found by Yellow Horse, whose wife had just lost a child.

'My, you have led an exciting life!' Jo allowed, smiling. 'And Grandfather taught you the whiteman's way of life and cared for you?'

'More or less.' He hesitated, saw them both watching him closely, then made up his mind and told them about the Rocking R ranch and how Noble had wanted to help him claim his rightful legacy.

'But Kent don't want that,' he concluded. 'Had his hired gun leave me for dead in the desert, but luckily I remembered an old Indian trail and a bunch returning from a lion hunt found me. . . .'

'And, despite all your personal troubles, you took the risk of going back to recover the gold. Then delivered it: to us!' Jo shook her head in wonderment. 'You are indeed a man of your word, Mr Fargo!'

'Name's Lee – leastways, that's the one I'm going by right now. According to Sam my real name is Gideon Rockwell, but I guess I'll never prove that now.'

His genuine regret brought a small silence.

'Pity,' Kyle said, and then looked sharply at Jo as he caught the expression on her face. 'Sis. . . ?'

'I was thinking. Mr Far— Lee has gone to a great deal of trouble on our behalf. . . .'

'No trouble, ma'am, really.'

Her smile warmed him.

'We appreciate everything you've done, Lee. Kyle, you were only complaining over breakfast that you have so little work – people aren't sure about your abilities right now – here is a grand opportunity for you to show them just how good an attorney you can be.'

He frowned a little deeper, then looked startled. 'You mean—?'

'Yes!' the girl cut in excitedly. 'Take up Lee's fight to claim his legacy from this Kent Rockwell. The gold here will pay expenses and if we're successful, then Lee can reimburse you.'

'Well, sure,' Fargo said a little hesitantly, looking from one to the other, 'but what if you – we – lose? You'll be out of pocket because I won't have any way of paying you.'

'That's the risk every attorney takes on a case like this,' Kyle said, somewhat distractedly: it was clear he was running over Jo's suggestion in his mind. 'Really the first thing to do is to establish your real identity, Lee. I'm not sure that's going to be easy now that Granddad isn't around to tell his story. Is there anyone else who could swear that you're Gideon Rockwell?'

'I'm not sure – Sam told me there's a woman who lives in Waco, called Rosa Reynola – he said she's my birth mother.'

'Then there you are!' Jo said excitedly. 'If you can bring her back here— Kyle, why are you looking like that?'

'The woman's word may not be enough, Sis, we'll need papers – birth certificate – marriage certificate and so on. She may well have these, of course, I hope she does, but even if we establish Lee as Gideon, we could still have trouble claiming a half-share in Rocking R.'

That silenced them and they finished their coffee and Fargo had a second cup. For a few minutes there he had been hopeful, but, deep down, he could only forsee heaps of trouble, perhaps years of court cases. *Hell, nothing had been easy in his life so far: this wasn't likely to be any different.*

'You *do* want to claim your legacy, don't you, Lee?' asked the girl. 'You don't seem enthusiastic.'

'I guess I'm out of my depth. But I want to find Rosa; I guess that's the starting point. And however things turn out, I aim to square with Kent for murdering Brent.'

'That's perfectly understandable,' Kyle allowed. 'But Rosa might have a copy of Brent's Will, naming you as legatee, and that'll be an immense help.'

Fargo shrugged, shook his head. 'I guess I can ask. But, Kyle, you sure you really want to do this?'

'I do, Lee! I truly do! I can read between the lines of your story, how Granddad was implicated in leaving you – how shall we say? – adrift in the wilderness. . . ? But he took the trouble to rescue you later when he realized who you were, acquainted you with the whiteman's way of life, and intended to help you claim your birthright. Whether he hoped to earn some reward for himself makes no difference. I feel I'm obligated to help you and I *want* to help you, Lee. Apart from the challenge, that legacy is rightfully yours.'

He thrust out a hand and Fargo gripped after a slight hesitation. Jo smiled and moved towards a sideboy where a golden liquid sat in a cut-glass decanter, surrounded by matching glasses. She began to pour three drinks.

'Gentlemen, I give you a toast – to the Brazos Legacy. May it soon come home to roost!'

They drank to that.

There were six riders in the group thundering over the arched wooden bridge that crossed the Colorado River heading out of Austin.

Kent Rockwell rode out front with Rip Ohlrig on his right. Behind were the four hardcases, including Chick Sawtell, all chosen by Kent himself.

'Would've been quicker to take the stage,' Ohlrig griped as dust swirled up around his head. He tugged up his neckerchief over mouth and nostrils.

'You heard the Wells, Fargo clerk in Austin – trail's washed away up ahead at Monroe Bend,' snapped Rockwell, just as tired and irritable from the long ride. 'Might or might not be cleared by the time the stage is due to leave, We can't wait around any longer. We've lost enough time already.'

'You can't be sure Fargo'll go to San Antone,' Rip growled. 'Hell, with a few pokes of gold he might just head for the bright lights, a long ways from here.'

Rockwell shook his head. 'No, Gann was speakin' gospel. I know Sam's wife lived in San Antone after she run out on Sam. There was a daughter who could've had a couple growed-up kids by now . . . anyway, we've got the names. We can look.'

'And if he ain't there?'

Rockwell shot a bleak glance at Ohlrig.

'Then we look someplace else – and this time we keep lookin' till we find him. And I *see* the son of a bitch die with a bullet in his head!'

Ohlrig ran a tongue around his dry lips under the neckerchief.

Yeah! He had that to live with! First time ever he hadn't delivered on a job he was paid to do. It would be a matter of pride to put things right now.

A matter of pride. . . .

The deputy sheriff Fargo spoke to in Waco knew the Reynolas all right.

'They was here for a few years – he's an Indian Agent, you know, part Mex. Nice enough feller, was transferred to the Falcone Reservation just over a year back. You know it? In the foothills leadin' to the Edwards Plateau, not far from San Marco.'

'Heard of it. I'll find my way there. Thanks. Can I buy you a beer?'

'Only one on duty; can't leave the office. But if ever you're passin' through again. . . .'

'It's a deal.'

Fargo shook hands, went to a general store and, using some money that Jo and Kyle had insisted he take for travelling expenses, bought stores for the long trail to the reservation.

He arrived just on dark. It was raining again and he was muddy and cold and wet beneath his new poncho.

Shivering, he knocked on the door of the agent's quarters that had been pointed out to him by one of the surly reservation police.

A light was burning inside and a honey-skinned girl in pigtails, about ten years old, opened the door and stared at him with large brown eyes.

He nodded and water cascaded from the curl brim of his hat. She jumped back, laughing, to avoid being splashed.

He grinned. 'Sorry, *señorita.* I'm looking for Señora Reynola.'

The girl turned from him without speaking, ran back down a short hallway and disappeared through a door.

He waited, listening to the rain hammering on the shingles of the porch roof above him, water dribbling through and pattering against the stiff brim of his hat. Then a woman came slowly down the passage, looking curiously at him as she approached – a woman in her mid-forties, a little overweight, perhaps, but her face still retained some of her past striking beauty, although she looked careworn. She wiped her hands on an apron tied about her waist and nodded to him.

'I can help you, *señor*? I am Rosa Reynola. . . .'

He stared, suddenly tongue-tied, his mind a'swirl with a hundred, no a *thousand* colliding thoughts. *This woman was his mother and he didn't even know what to say to her!*

His heart pounded furiously as he searched for the right words.

'*Señor*?' She sounded a little wary now, backed-up a step, and he knew she was becoming agitated.

Then, without conscious thought, he blurted, 'I'm your son – Gideon Rockwell.'

Her jaw dropped. Her eyes widened.

Then she crumpled and he just managed to catch her and lower her gently to the floor as she passed out in a dead faint.

13

Bullets & Bows

The train arrived ten hours late in San Antonio. The rain had caused a wash-away down the track at Candlewick Pass, all the blue metal being torn from under several sections of rails by the muddy waters. The engineer refused to take his train over unsupported track. Luckily there were two wagons of trimmed poles on a siding, awaiting transport on the special Western Union train to the big camp up at Piute Mesa where they were stringing a new telegraph line.

Lucky in one way: not so lucky for the male passengers. Because they all had to get out and lend a hand, rolling the logs across and working them under the sagging sections of rail at intervals until the Irish engineer was satisfied they would support the locomotive and cars. By that time the rain had eased and eventually the train got going again. But it was a wise precaution, although it later caused the devil of a row between the railroad and Western Union.

But none of that concerned Lee Fargo. He was just anxious to get back to Kyle and Jo and give them the news he carried. His clothes were muddy and his hands were sore and raw from handling the logs, but the manual work had helped ease some of the tension that had been building within him since leaving Falcone. Shouldering his warbag, the skies still threatening, he hurried out towards Mission Street. It was past nine o'clock and the night wind was chill as he slogged through muddy puddles to the end of the street.

He was glad to see a light burning in the Preston house and started towards it. Rain water had cut a channel across the yard and forced him to swing wide so that he was actually approaching a back corner of the house when the kitchen door opened and a man stepped up to the stoop and began to urinate.

Fargo stopped in his tracks, crouching, the old Comanche ways coming instinctively. It wasn't young Kyle. The man was too big and sloppily dressed. He hawked and spat, buttoned his trousers and, as he turned to go back inside and close the door, the light washed across him. He was hatless and although his face was only revealed very briefly, Fargo recognized him at once.

Chick Sawtell.

Now what in hell's name was that hardcase doing here?

He swung towards the house, carrying the warbag in his arms now. He propped it against the wall, decided it would be best to use the sixgun. He freed it from the wet holster, then wiped mud and grit from the barrel and the bulge of the cylinder with his shirt tail. He worked the hammer smoothly several times, with trigger depressed so that the ratchet wouldn't engage, and made his way around the corner to the rear of the house.

Crouching, he looked in the steamed-up window of the kitchen, the frame outlined by the dull glow of the lamp inside. Everything was blurred, but he could make out Chick Sawtell all right. Sitting at the deal table, a sawn-off shotgun close to his hand, he played solitaire, a bored expression on his long, lantern-jawed face.

He suddenly flung the cards down on to the table with a curse that Fargo heard clearly. 'I need a goddamn drink and there ain't a single shot of redeye in this dump!' Chick said, standing fast enough to knock over the chair with a clatter. The noise didn't seem to bother Chick, and Fargo felt the knot in his belly tighten as he wondered what had happened to Kyle and Jo . . . they should've heard that!

Whatever it was, it didn't bother Sawtell.

But if he was going for a drink, then Fargo had to intercept him and find out what had happened here.

He was waiting when the hardcase came out the front door, leaving it open, the house now dark behind him. He hitched up his pants, hawked into the night and stumbled as he came down the front steps. Fargo came out of the shadows and struck with his gun barrel, crashing it behind Chick's left ear. . . .

When Sawtell came round, he was slumped in a kitchen chair and the lamp was burning on the table again, the spilled cards shining in its light. But the shine that caught his eye most was the one that came from his own sawn-off shotgun, held loosely in Fargo's hands, the man sitting opposite him across the table.

'Where're the Prestons, Chick?' asked Fargo mildly.

Sawtell had to shake his head a little to clear his senses and he moaned, put up a hand and felt the sticky blood oozing from the knot behind his ear.

'You son of a bitch!'

One hand rested on the edge of the table, Fargo struck like a snake. The heavy barrels of the shotgun mashed Chick's fingers and he howled as he snatched his hand against his chest, swearing. Fargo reached out a long, lazy leg and pushed. Chick's chair went over backwards and he sprawled, frowning: this was a new Fargo, much harder, with a merciless look in his eye that made Chick's bowels quake.

'Where're the Prestons?' he asked again, quietly.

The expression on the young man's face really bothered Chick. It wasn't so much an ugly thing as it was terrifying – and *that* was a new sensation. He recognized it as a kind of savagery, almost animal, a totally merciless look he had seen on the faces of blood-crazed Indians. He knew he was in a *lot* of trouble here. . . .

He swallowed. 'They're OK.'

Fargo kicked him in the face, just a snapping motion of his leg from the knee down, but it put the struggling Chick flat on his back again, blood at his nostrils and mouth. He spat a broken tooth.

'*Jesus!*'

Fargo pinned him with his stare and covered him with the shotgun. Then, biting back the pain, Sawtell spoke, his words slurred, 'Kent's got 'em. There's an

old swing-station outside of town at Battle Creek, fallin'
down since the railroad came an'—'

This time he just managed to dodge Fargo's boot
and, sprawling on his side, eyes wide, he lifted one hand
protectively across his face. 'Take it easy! I'll tell you
what happened.'

Mickey Gann had spilled his guts about the gold and
where Fargo was taking it. Rockwell had decided to put
an end to the whole thing, came here with a hardcase
crew.

'Kent left me here to tell you he wants you to ride out
there, unarmed, and – well, he'll take it from there.'

'He aim to kill the Prestons?'

Chick hesitated and Fargo read the answer in his
eyes. He stood abruptly and Chick cringed as the shotgun barrels swung down in his direction.

'The world'll be a better place without Kent
Rockwell,' Fargo told him quietly. '*And* his men. I
s'pose Ohlrig's with him?' Chick nodded. 'Who else?'

'Just Rip.'

Fargo saw the way he gathered himself, ready for
another kick, and he knew the man was lying. 'You're
not a helluva lot of use, either, Chick – you on that raid
at Eliza Creek?'

Sawtell didn't want to answer but eventually he
nodded. 'Uh-huh – thought as much,' Fargo said. 'Well,
guess I got no use for you at all, Chick. So long, you
murdering son of a bitch.'

The charge of buckshot blew Sawtell across the small
kitchen, his body skidding to a halt at the base of the
wood-burning stove. Fargo tossed the smoking gun

down beside him.

He doubted the shot would have been heard above the rain-laden wind, this far from town. Not that he cared one way or the other. Truth was, there wasn't a hell of a lot he did care about right now, except saving the Prestons, seeing as he had been the one to bring them trouble in the first place.

He took Chick's big grey horse which he found still saddled in the stables out back, changed into his buckskins, slinging the bow case and quiver of arrows across his back as he rode off. It was several miles to the Battle Creek swing-station and long before he reached it he came to the creek itself, walked the horse out into the shallow waters. He followed it to where the willows whipping in the wind told him he had reached the bend where the ford was. The old adobe swing-station lay just beyond.

They wouldn't be expecting him to come from this direction, but they would likely have a man watching just as a precaution. He tethered the horse under the willows, kept his sixgun buckled about his waist but left the rifle. He slung the quiver on to his back after taking the bow out of its case and stringing it swiftly. It was a short horse bow, only about forty-two inches long, but very powerful. In Rumpled Hair's younger days he had killed hundreds of buffalo with this bow from the back of a thundering cayuse: he had seldom needed more than two arrows, often only using one. His exploits were still told around the tribal and reservation camp-fires.

Fargo nocked an arrow, standing in the deep shadows of the whispering willows, letting his eyes search the

darkness. The peeling white adobe of the station building seemed to glow in the strange light as thunderheads
roiled and swirled across the sky, blotting out the stars.
There were no lamps burning, of course, but he did see
the red coal of a cigarette against the wall near the
main door.

Standing perfectly still, moving only his eyes and
using his peripheral vision for better resolution, he
scanned the ground between the creek and the building. There was a hollow thirty yards away, its deeper
shadow marking it. As he watched, something broke
the blurred outline and it took him only seconds to
realize it was a man's head, then his shoulders as he
stood up, stretching the cramps out of his aching body.

Whoever he was, he died that way. An arrow cleft the
night and impaled him through the chest.

As another arrow nocked on to the animal-tendon
string with a brief, almost inaudible, drumming sound,
Fargo crouched double and moved, still within the
deepest shadow, closer to the station building.

'Buck! *Buck*!'

Fargo stopped dead, one foot raised, balanced
perfectly, his heart jumping as a man called his pard's
name from only a few yards ahead. He must have heard
the *thump!* of the arrow as it tore into the man in the
hollow.

'Buck, what the hell was that?' he called again, in a
hoarse whisper that carried across the yard.

'Shut up, Slim!' someone hissed over to Fargo's right
– the man he had seen earlier with the cigarette.

Then Slim, just in front of Fargo, muttered a curse

and said clearly, 'Damnit! *I heard something*!'

'You'll hear Rip kickin' your teeth in you don't shut up!' hissed that voice to the right again.

The man murmured grumpily to himself and then Fargo drew the bow and the arrow sped silently through the night and the Rocking R man never knew what hit him.

Fargo laid the bow on the ground and, knife in hand now, moved like a snake over to the right. A minute later the man with the cigarette was lying on his back, gurgling as his life's blood bubbled out of the gash in his throat.

Fargo rolled behind a log, sliding the bloody blade into its beaded sheath.

Chick had said there were only three others besides himself and Rockwell and Rip Ohlrig. But Fargo scouted all around the adobe building before he was satisfied there were no more men waiting in ambush.

Then he heard a scream from the stage-station, swiftly muffled, and he leapt to his feet and ran towards the old building, reaching for his sixgun.

A rifle began firing from one of the low front windows, the bullets searching for him, kicking stones and dust. *Someone in there had cat's eyes!*

Then he was spinning and rolling as a bullet ripped across his side and he heard pounding boots, glimpsed a dark shape rising against the darker shapes of the clouds. He tried to roll on to his side, groping for his sixgun that he had dropped when he fell.

Then there was an explosion of light as a rifle butt crashed between his eyes. . . .

*

He came round sprawled in a corner of the stage-station, dried blood from a gash at his hairline making his left eye sticky and hard to open. He rubbed it free and looked around him, pain knifing briefly low down on his left side.

There was a lantern set on the edge of an old bench and its light revealed Kyle and Jo Preston huddled in a corner along the same wall as his own. It also showed Rip Ohlrig and Kent Rockwell, both sitting on upturned packing cases, Ohlrig holding a pistol, Kent nursing a rifle.

'Are you all right, Lee?' Jo asked concernedly.

He nodded and grimaced as pain soared through his side. His brain felt loose inside his skull. He lifted his gaze to the rancher and his hardcase.

'Had you figured right,' Kent said, with a smug satisfaction. 'Rip put you down as just another Injun gone bad – me, I said, no, he's mebbe more Injun than white but there's enough of Brent in him for him to risk his stupid neck just to save these here Preston kids – and I was right!'

'Wrong,' grated Fargo, and he savoured the couple of seconds when the startled, puzzled look crossed the rancher's face. 'There's nothing of Brent in me, Rockwell. What I do, I do because that's the way I am.'

Kent curled a lip. 'Have it your way then. Makes no nevermind . . . you're not gonna be around for much longer.'

'I had *that* figured,' Fargo told him, coming out of

his daze rapidly now, but not letting on too much. He deliberately slurred his words, but he saw that Rip wasn't fooled. He was alert and ready for instant trouble. 'OK, you've got me – so turn loose Kyle and Jo. They were just showing their gratitude for me bringing 'em the gold old Sam had been putting away for 'em.'

Kent Rockwell almost smiled.

'Yeah, how 'bout that? Ol' Sam got a couple thousand bucks' worth together over the years. Dunno where he found it, but it was cached on my land so it's finder's keepers far as I'm concerned.'

'That was the Prestons' legacy from Sam!' Fargo said. 'He busted a gut grubbing for that gold!'

'Too bad! You think I'm gonna let 'em have it? Or you think the Rockin' R is gonna be *your* legacy?'

'Sam thought so. He convinced me, and I went along with him because he'd saved my neck, but I wasn't sure I wanted a ranch. Or even half a one.'

'Still missin' your Injun pards?' chuckled Rip. 'Hell, how anyone calls hisself white can stand their stink sure beats the hell outa me.'

'Funny, Rip, they always say a whiteman stinks.'

'Well, a dead man stinks pretty much the same, whether he's red *or* white – an' you'll be dead right soon, Fargo!'

'Stop all this talk of killing! Please!' Jo was plainly upset but her hazel eyes were hard and defiant as she looked at Ohlrig. 'You just can't get away with cold-blooded murder, don't you realize that?'

Ohlrig chuckled. 'Guess I don't, 'cause I been gettin'

away with it for years! Looks like I'll have to mend my ways, Kent!'

'Start tomorrow, Rip,' Rockwell said, still with his smugness.

'Yeah, I'll do that. Have one last fling tonight – just say when, Kent.'

Rockwell sighed, ran his eyes over Fargo, then looked at the Prestons. 'Yeah, well, might as well get it done – We're way past talkin'.'

'Maybe not,' Fargo said, and all eyes turned to him.

'You got anythin' to say, you better do it quick,' Kent said curtly. 'I'm runnin' outa patience. Far as I'm concerned it all ends here and now.'

'Well, it could,' Fargo allowed, 'but something has come up that might interest you.'

Rockwell looked bored. 'And what would that be?'

Fargo flicked his eyes from Rockwell to Ohlrig to the Prestons. But he was looking straight at the rancher when he said flatly, 'Thing is, none of this is necessary.'

'That so?' Rockwell sounded faintly amused. 'And how come it suddenly ain't *necessary* for me to protect my interest – and Liza's – in Rockin' R?'

Fargo's eyes didn't waver. 'Because I'm not Gideon Rockwell.'

The words fell into the shadowy room like heavy stones falling into a shallow pool, splashing all those around the edge with sudden cold shock.

Fargo actually felt the intensity of their gazes as they all looked at him.

'I saw Rosa Reynola up at Falcone. She fainted dead away when I told her I was Gideon – not because I'd suddenly turned up on her doorstep, but because she doesn't believe in ghosts – and that's what I'd have to be if I *was* Gideon. He died in Yellow Horse's camp before he was a year old – some kind of fever. There was a captive white woman in the same camp who gave birth to a boy child right afterwards. She died but the kid lived. Yellow Horse figured white babies bad medicine by then, having caused so much grief for his wife, so he tied that silver dollar around the new baby's neck and gave him to a Kiowa squaw. Later, she gave him to another Comanche woman, because her husband hated all whites and she was afraid he might kill the kid – which was me.'

There was a brief silence, then Kyle asked quietly, 'How – how d'you know all this, Lee?'

'Rosa. She searched for Gideon for years. She was able to get in touch with plenty of Indians because she married an Indian agent. It took her a long time, but she found the right tribe eventually – the People of the Desert Eagle, under Chief Rumpled Hair. They reared me, but most were wiped out by the army after Custer's massacre. That's when Sam Noble found me and thought I was Gideon. I was about the right age and I had that silver dollar that Brent had made – Rosa showed me Brent's Will and Gideon was to inherit a half-share in Rocking R, right enough, but now it'll never matter, Kent, because you murdered Brent, Gideon's dead and me – well, I dunno *who* I am.'

There was a bitter, lost, edge to his voice as he concluded.

'Oh, Lee!' Jo was genuinely sympathetic despite her

own predicament and she started to her feet to go to
Fargo.

Both Kent and Ohlrig were still a little stunned by
what Fargo had told them and they reacted just a mite
too slowly.

They both turned to the girl at once, shouting, and
then Fargo was upon them, hurling himself in a head-
long dive, arms spread so that he knocked both men off
their feet at the same time.

He drove a moccasined foot ino Rip's face, snapping
the man's head back. Ohlrig slammed hard into the
adobe and Jo gave a small cry, knocked flying by his
outflung arm, cannoning into her brother who was also
rising to his feet. They went down in a tangle and
suddenly Kent's rifle blasted and showered them with
adobe as the bullet tore a long furrow across the wall.

Out of the thrashing human pile came Fargo,
squirming free, Rip Ohlrig's pistol in his hand. Kent
was on one knee, face wild and dark with rage,
fumbling the lever of the rifle as Fargo dropped flat and
the Colt thundered three times. The bullets hurled
Kent back across the room and he jarred violently
against the wall, legs buckling. He dropped to his
knees, hands fluttering in front of his bleeding chest,
and then toppled forward and spread out on his face.

'Lee!' bawled Kyle urgently, and Fargo rolled away,
spinning on to his side, the Colt dragging around
through the dirt and straw on the floor.

Rip, nose bleeding, had Kent's rifle in his big hands
as he bared his teeth, braced the butt into his hip and
triggered. At the same moment, Fargo fired and flung

himself back, wrenching the bullet burn in his side but hardly noticing any pain.

Rip Ohlrig's body was lifted clear off the ground by the bullet smashing into the middle of his brutal face. Jo quickly covered her eyes and Kyle clasped her to his chest, his own face grimacing in horror as Ohlrig splashed gore across the adobe wall before falling like a heap of rags on the floor. . . .

Fargo calmed Kyle and Jo down, then threw a saddle blanket over the bodies, dragging them outside.

'Lee, I'm so sorry how things worked out – for you,' Jo Preston said sadly when he returned. She washed the bullet wound in his side while he sat stripped to the waist on an upturned packing case. 'I mean – not knowing who you are – it must be awful.'

He nodded, tight-lipped. 'Ought to be used to it by now. Seems I've never known who I really am. It used to worry me when I was living with the Indians. I didn't remember anything of my mother, of course. All my memories were of life with the tribe, but they never let me forget I was white and I just had to wonder if I had any kinfolk amongst the Texans. I was only a kid and didn't know what to do or think – so I just pushed it to the back of my mind. Then Sam found me and more or less dragged me into the white world. It scared me, which was why I ran off a few times. I went back to the Indians and I became a blooded warrior riding with a war party against some Pawnee. It was exciting but – I wondered how I'd feel when we killed whites. All the conflict inside me started again. So when Sam tracked me down I went with him and tried to fit in with the whites.'

'Sam used you, Lee, you see that, don't you?' Kyle said gently. 'He wanted to get back at Kent for lying to him all those years, keeping him around, letting him think he was a wanted man – and during that time his wife died and his daughter, our mother, married a worthless man. You were to be the instrument of Sam's revenge, no matter what he told you about claiming the legacy.'

'I know; I figured all that out. But that don't bother me, never did, really,' broke in Fargo. 'I owed Sam. If he hadn't taken me that first time, I would've been killed when the army massacred most of the tribe. But now—' He paused and they waited in silence, watching his face: mixture of sadness, bewilderment and a new determination. 'I *still* dunno where I belong, or who I am.'

'Some white children were stolen in a Comanche raid on Biggsville about the time Gideon was taken, Lee,' Kyle said with an edge of excitement. 'You may have been one of them – I could start enquiries.'

Fargo shook his head. 'No, Kyle, though much obliged for the offer. Most of Biggesville was wiped out. My mother died amongst the Indians. Even if we came up with a possible name, there'd be no one left who'd be interested in me. That'd seem somehow worse than this uncertainty.'

'It's an awful predicament, Lee,' Jo said, her eyes moist as she tied off the bandage. 'What will you do?'

'I think I might go up into the mountains. . . .'

It was two weeks before Lee Fargo showed up again at the Preston house in San Antonio.

Kyle and Jo were sitting on the porch, going through some legal papers to do with a court case that Kyle was working on when they heard a horse in the timber across the vacant lot.

At first they didn't recognize him – he was wearing buckskins. There was a single brown-barred eagle feather held in place at the back of his head by a rawhide band painted with symbols. They thought he *was* an Indian at first sight.

But he looked different – younger, Jo thought. No, not just younger – more serene. . . .

He had come to terms with something!

They didn't know and he didn't explain, but he had gone into the Brazos Hills, spent four days purifying himself in a sweat lodge he built on a rocky ledge high on a mountain peak, as close to the sky as he could get. Using white clay as a sign of purity, he dabbed it upon his naked body in the patterns shown to him by the Desert Eagle tribe's *shaman* long ago, when he had been twelve years old.

At that time, he had been sent alone into wild country with the skull of a buffalo, painted with celestial and mystic signs. Cold, hungry, afraid, and clasping a bunch of sacred sage, he had entreated the Great Spirit to send him a vision – and he had seen the shadow of an eagle chasing a long-legged timber wolf. Thereafter he had been named Tall Wolf. The shaman had foretold that he would leave the tribe one day and when he returned he would be a great leader.

Fargo had tried to forget these things after he had finally settled into the whiteman's way of life, but now –

after seeing Rosa – he decided he would try the Indian way once more, searching inside himself for a vision of true meaning that would give him direction – and peace.

This time he had asked the Great Spirit for his identity, his true name. Of course, no name had been forthcoming, but he had felt a surge of knowledge that while he might never know who he really was, somehow it didn't matter so much now. *For he had learned a great truth: he was already whatever the Great Spirit had made him: that was what counted . . . and what he did on his chosen path through life.*

A new vision came this time, in much greater clarity than before. Once again there was a desert eagle, but showing every feather and marking, no longer just a shadow without detail. There was a howling wolf in its talons as it soared higher and higher, climbing into the sky . . . towards the sun.

Very good medicine indeed!

As Jo and Kyle waved to him now, eager for his company, he stood in his stirrups and held high Rumpled Hair's bow in one hand. 'I now know who I am!' he called.

The Prestons were genuinely pleased and Jo clapped her hands. 'I'm so glad for you, Lee! Or do you have another name now?'

Still standing in the stirrups, the horse moving a little with impatience, he called, 'I am Tall Wolf, of the People of the Desert Eagle. There are few of my tribe left now. I go to find them and spend my life with them. I am Tall Wolf – farewell, *amigos.*'

Jo and Kyle were stunned. 'Oh, *please* come back some day!' Jo cried, as Tall Wolf slung the bow on his back.

'He – he's going Indian again!' Kyle said.

Then Jo smiled faintly. 'No, I don't think so, Kyle. I think he's going *back*. It's really the only life he's known. He just didn't fit in with the whites – I think this is his true legacy. . . .'

Kyle said nothing as Tall Wolf settled into the saddle, turned the big horse and rode away from San Antone, heading out across the rolling plains towards the distant purple haze shrouding the beckoning mountains that were the beginning of Comanche country.

They watched until the dust settled and they could see him no more.